MW01231828

FROM SOMETHING BAD

FROM

SOMETHING

BAD

LT LEWIS

From Something Bad
Copyright © 2020 by LT Lewis

Cover and interior design by Lance Buckley
www.lancebuckley.com

All rights reserved. No part of this book may be reproduced
or used in any manner without written permission of the author
except for the use of quotations in a book review.

For Adam S.

WASHINGTON, D.C. 1993

A cacophony of angry car horns, spewed like insults, slipped through the rusted bars of a cast iron fence and drifted over a four-foot-deep concrete moat before passing through the curtain-less window of Troy Hunter's street level studio. Naked and comatose, Troy lay on the carpeted floor of the empty apartment. A chilled sweat coated his torso while the lower half of his body was cocooned in a red down sleeping bag, dank with the smell of urine. Riding the swells of his labored breaths was a chrome-plated .38 revolver, cold and oily against his bare chest, like a sleeping reptile.

It was night when Troy surfaced from his delirium and he lay perfectly still, savoring the sluggish return of his senses. Fractals of light shed from the headlamps of passing traffic flitted across the empty walls reminding Troy of another night, long ago, when he was just a boy. The place was Good Time Charlie's, a seedy strip club stashed away in the back pocket of *The Combat Zone*, Boston's infamous red light district. Troy, then sixteen years old and drunk for the first time, sat in a VIP booth, squeezed between Marvin the pimp and his entourage of oversized goons.

Troy sipped from a can of Schlitz, his fourth of the night. The beer was warm and flat but well worth the pleasant buzz he'd been riding for the past half-hour. Equally pleasant was its analgesic effect, and he touched his left eye, swollen shut, while his right eye continued to greedily mind the half-naked dancer who worked the stage. Suspended high above by a wire and illuminated like a celestial orb from a puppet-sized universe, was a glittering disco ball. It twirled slowly and with an equanimity that Troy found comforting, its hundreds of tiny mirrors showering the room with a capricious dance of colored lights.

A chill washed over Troy and he yanked at the edges of his sleeping bag sending an electric shock through his wrists, the pain trivial compared to the headaches which came in waves and with little warning. It was the same each time. First it was the fever, turning his body into a human furnace, his breath so hot it nearly singed the hairs in his nose. His eyes bubbled in their sockets like poached eggs and then a dull throb appeared at the base of his neck, followed by a growing pressure that tugged at the sutures of his skull. Finally, rigors, his entire body shaking uncontrollably, and just when he felt he couldn't stand any of it one second more, everything went dark.

He squeezed his eyes shut and tried to steer his mind away from his own predicament and towards the life that was going on just outside his window. He forced himself to concentrate on the sounds drifting through window: the hum of trolling taxis; the stuttering clank of a drill coming from somewhere across town; the hiss of an espresso machine from a cafe just across the street; and the faint gurgle of voices. Troy focused on the unintelligible speech, and then one voice seemed to break free and rise above the others, and as if he had turned the knob of a radio tuner, the unintelligible prattle crystallized into a familiar voice.

"The only free man is the man who has everything and the man who has nothing," Brother Nathan said. "Which one you gonna be, Troy?"

And then Troy could see Brother Nathan as clear as yesterday, pacing back and forth in a turtleneck and leather jacket, the signature black beret threatening to slide off a black head, bald as a knee cap. "What's it gonna be, little soldier?"

Poor Brother Nate, Troy thought. If life had ever miscast anyone, it was Brother Nate, duped into playing the role of an angry black man, but in secret, an avid reader of *Mad Magazine*; a fan of Johnny Carson, Bob Dylan, the Red Sox and Steve McQueen movies. No real fire. No anger. Just fear.

Nate had been wrong about so many things, Troy told himself. *The only free man was the man without a life, without a past, without a role to act out for the little time one had in this world.*

Or did I give up? Troy wondered.

Troy tried to shake the thought from his head. It rattled about his skull like a broken filament in a light bulb until a different voice spoke, but this time Troy was expecting it.

"You gave up, Troy. You plain gave up."

Coming from Reverend Jones, who once wandered the planet like a sadistic missionary, asking strangers when they gave up on life and decided to be so average, it was the ultimate insult.

"Do you remember that moment? Do you remember what you were doing at the precise moment when you gave up your dreams?" he'd say, as if asking where you were when Kennedy was shot, or the space shuttle *Challenger* disappeared from our TV screens in a tiny puff of smoke. And then snot-nosed Lou would slap the back of his hand against his forehead, and making an L with his thumb and forefinger, begin *mooing* the word *loser* like a sick cow. *Looo ooo ser.*

Had Troy stayed the course, he might still be hanging with Lou in Manhattan, still wearing hand-tailored suits, and still working for the man with the humongous teeth, the man they called, among other things, *the master puppeteer.*

Those fucking teeth! Troy thought. A million years from now, after the apes had taken control of the planet, Dr. Zaius would hold the skull of the man with the humongous teeth in his hairy palms and decide that this long extinct creature was a carnivore, and that the oversized teeth were used to tear the hearts out of his fellow man, and he would be right.

But after a brief stint in the corporate world, Troy left to get the education he was denied that day, over twenty years ago, when

Brother Nate had plucked him from the flatlands of Oakland and sent him three thousand miles east.

I've seen things you people wouldn't believe, Troy thought, recalling a line from a favorite sci-fi movie.

"But what have you learned, Troy?" asked the Reverend.

Learned? Troy thought, and suddenly he was thirteen years-old again, sitting at the oval shaped wooden table in a musky class room in the basement of the Academy Building while the mammoth preacher stroked his chin, and, along with eleven other classmates, waited for his answer. Troy wanted to answer—knew exactly what he wanted to say—but he couldn't make the words leave his lips. The classroom of children giggled and the Reverend sighed and shook his head.

Troy was sweating profusely now, every gland, every orifice, straining to dissipate heat. A familiar pressure settled at the base of his skull, not quite pain, but uncomfortable, and he grasped his head between his palms and squeezed his temples, slick with sweat.

No more. Please, no more! Troy pleaded as the pressure grew. A few moments longer and the shakes would start.

"Time is running out, son. Have you found it?" asked the Reverend. "Have you found something to believe in?"

Troy pushed himself up into a sitting position, spilling the pistol onto the floor.

He stared at the gun, noticing for the first time, the etching in the pistol's walnut grip. He lifted it up for a closer look. Carved into the wood were concentric rings, evenly spaced, nine in all.

The gun grew heavy, his hand trembling under the weight, and another memory bubbled to the surface, this one older than the last. He and Brother Nate, shoulder to shoulder, riding the *Alpine Racer* rollercoaster at Playland in Ocean Beach. Their train jerked and stuttered as it climbed the rickety wooden tracts high above the amusement park.

It was a windy day, a spotless blue sky swept clean of all clouds, and Troy, his heart racing, stared down at the shrinking beach goers with their white swimming trunks and tan bodies. Foam dipped waves spilled lazily onto the beach, pausing for just a moment before being sucked back into the ocean, like the breath of sleeping giant.

As their train reached the top, it wrenched to a stop just long enough for Troy to grasp the inevitability of the plunge before him. Fear replaced excitement as the train teetered on the summit, trying to decide which way to go. Finally, the weight of the train tipped forward and they began to fall. Troy closed his eyes and reached for Nate's hand and squeezed, but felt only on the unforgiving wood of the pistol's grip.

The pressure at the base of Troy's neck was back and building with a momentum that couldn't be stopped. He knew he had only seconds left before the rigors would start, stripping Troy of control over his own body.

He looped his index finger over the gun's trigger.

"Troy? Troy?" the Reverend called out, his voice drowned out by the pain in his skull.

"I'm sorry," Troy whispered, shaking his head, his eyes clenched shut like two balled fists. "Please forgive me."

He cocked the gun's hammer and pressed the mouth of the barrel to his chin.

"*Pater, peccavi*," Troy whispered.

PART ONE

1969
OAKLAND, CALIFORNIA

Through the keyhole of his bedroom door, Troy observed Leon's skinny legs dangling off the edge of the living room couch. He watched patiently, and when three minutes passed and Leon had not moved, Troy pressed his ear up against the same keyhole, his eyes shut in deep concentration. He could hear Leon's breath, the heavy panting of a sleeping animal. One last peek through the keyhole to make sure his legs had not moved and then Troy was out of his room, tip toeing past the sleeping Leon, towards the front door. As he passed the back of the tattered couch, he peered down at the mossy stubble overgrowing Leon's haggard face connecting his long sideburns to his pointy chin. Although Leon's eyes were closed, Troy knew better than to let his guard down. He could see the empty syringes on the coffee table, objects he had quickly learned to regard as danger signs; they meant when Leon awoke, he would be mean.

Please, please, don't wake up. Please, God, make him stay asleep.

Troy saw the sentinel quiver of Leon's lean body, a small quake before the seismic eruption.

"Who da fuck that?" Leon bellowed, his head coming up off the armrest of the sofa, which left a dent in his Afro.

Troy shrank back away from the couch as Leon's puffy blood-shot eyes darted about the room.

It was too late. Leon had seen him. Troy looked at the sweat stained sheet tented between Leon's legs where a two-day old erection refused to shrink.

"What da fuck you lookin' at? Where da fucks your mama?"

Troy smelled the mixture of sweat and urine emanating from the cloth couch where Leon had spent the last few days, and the stench made him want to vomit.

"Don't stand there retard, get me anuda amp."

"Troy late for school," Troy's mother said, appearing out of the kitchen just in time.

"Bitch, you gonna make a little girl outa him you keep protectin' him like dat. Beside, everyone know Troy a retard."

"Get on to school, Troy. You be late," his mother chastised.

Keeping his eyes on Leon, Troy scurried out the front door without a word.

Outside, Troy could finally breathe. It was one of those not unfamiliar California days, remarkable for its noticeable absence of weather: no wind, a cloudless blue sky and an impartial seventy-one degrees. Troy opened the short iron-gate of the Brookfield Village, turned left and continued briskly down Oak Street and then made another left onto Hyde Street.

Up ahead he could see the children gathering in front of the church in tight clusters, their book bags strewn carelessly on the white cement steps. Troy felt a certain amount of relief at the sight since this meant the doors to the church were still locked. He picked up the pace, half walking, half running, and when he was about fifty yards from the church, he saw the doors to the church swing inward and the mob of children begin to funnel inside. Troy had now broken out into a trot, his canvass book bag bouncing painfully off his right hip with every step.

Every morning before school, Troy ate breakfast at the St. Michael's Church, breakfast paid for and served-up by the *Black Panther Party for Self Defense* organization. After the children received their food, they spilled out into the main amphitheater of the church, sitting in pews, eating and talking with full mouths. The breakfast was offered to local school children of all ages but few high school kids ever showed up, most being too embarrassed to accept charity and acknowledge their family's poverty. The older kids who did show up came for the hot chocolate. They would drop Seconal tabs or *reds* as they were called, into the sweet hot liquid, swish it around until they melted, then gulp it all down. Troy was one of the only older kids who actually came for the breakfast.

As Troy stood in line, towering over most of the grade-schoolers, he tried to concentrate on the aluminum tin that held the bacon, but found his eye wondering away from the sizzling strips and on to the young woman doing the serving. Her hair was thick and natural, not straightened or treated in the style adopted by so many of the younger women. Pinned at a rakish angle to her Afro was a black beret. She wore black bellbottoms and a blue turtleneck and Troy eyes shifted from the bacon to the woman's large pointy breasts. Troy was no longer worrying about the status of bacon, his eyes full devouring the woman's body. Troy got his hash and eggs and stepped in front of the bacon tin.

"Hey, little soldier," she said, and Troy felt the familiar stirring in his pants. The woman dropped three strips of fatty bacon into Troy's plate. Troy mumbled a *thank you* before scurrying out of the classroom towards one of the less crowded pews in the rear of the church.

Troy ate slowly, the partial erection in his shorts subsiding even slower. As he ate, he watched two men talking behind the pulpit. One of the men Troy recognized as Reverend Joseph. The Reverend was a handsome older man, thin and sophisticated looking with neatly trimmed white hair. He always dressed in grey three-piece suits with the silver chain of a pocket watch looped from his vest. The Reverend kept smiling and shaking his head in disagreement to whatever it was the younger man was saying. The younger man was wearing the traditional panther garb—black pants, blue shirt, black leather jacket, and matching beret. His name was Brother Nathan. Troy didn't know much about Brother Nathan except that he was an important man in the neighborhood.

To Troy, Nathan looked anything but important. For one thing he was short—maybe five-foot four at most—with light skin and a shaved head. His eyes were protruding and bug-like and instead of black sunglasses, the young man wore rimless spectacles that seemed on the verge of slipping off his broad flat nose. He was anything but tough looking, unlike Leon who scared the shit out of Troy.

Troy's introduction to Leon was a memory he could never forget as much as he tried. Three months after Troy's father had been killed, Troy and his mother packed up their tiny white clapboard house in East Oakland and moved even further east to the Brookfield Village, a panther owned housing project. Two weeks later, Troy came home from school at two thirty in the afternoon as he did every day. He opened the front door with his own key, walked into the tiny living room of their new apartment and stopped frozen in his tracks. On the couch, three feet away from where he stood, was a writhing sandwich of black bodies.

His first reaction was confusion as to what he was seeing. It was definitely a man, his torso long and curved, with pointy hips bouncing off another body that was not visible, except for a pair of bare legs, which rose straight up on either side of the man. The man, who was panting loudly, hoisted himself into a push up stance and Troy gasped at the sight of his mother, naked and sweaty, lying beneath the stranger. The word *rape* popped into Troy's mind, a word he had heard many times, although he had no real idea of what it involved.

"Mamma!" Troy heard himself say.

"What da..shit!" the man yelled, jumping off Troy's mother.

Troy's mother sat up slowly. With the fingertips of one hand, she wiped the drops of sweat that had collected on the nipples of her large breasts. She was completely naked except for her silver hoop earrings and a row of silver bracelets coiled about one wrist, and Troy thought of the African women he'd seen in National Geographic magazines, bare chested with painted faces and skirts made from leaves and seashells strung together.

"Troy, go to your room. Your mama has a guest." Her voice was calm with maybe a trace of annoyance. Troy continued to look from his mother to the strange man who was still standing next to the couch staring at Troy in disbelief. He was tall and skinny and his penis seemed to point at Troy like big accusing finger.

"Troy!" his mother snapped.

Troy ran to his room and shut the door.

This was how Troy first met Leon who would become a permanent fixture in their tiny apartment over the next few years. As the months passed, the frightening incident was played over and over in Troy's mind. With both sadness and anger, Troy would recall his mother's annoyance at being disturbed. And three years later, when Brother Nathan offered Troy a chance to leave East Oakland for good, the image of his mother beneath Leon was the first to pop into Troy's mind, and what he remembered most was that after he fled to his room that day and shut the door, the panting and moaning resumed.

"School time, children," Reverend Joseph's voice boomed throughout the church. "Please empty your trays in the trash and stack them by the door on your way out."

Troy laid his green tray on the growing stack and stepped outside once again. Troy's favorite part of the day was now over and rest loomed ahead.

Two years ago, Troy was a labeled learning disabled by the Oakland Public School System, a label he had received from a psychology graduate student from Berkley who spent two weeks visiting the public schools of Oakland's flatlands as part of his fieldwork requirements. The psychology student, a white man of twenty-four, spent twenty minutes looking over teacher evaluations of Troy's last three school years, and determined from them (and his five minute meeting with Troy) that Troy had a learning disability. The "Impression" section of Troy's evaluation form read as follows:

Troy suffers from learning deficits concerning right-sided brain computations evidenced by Troy's difficulties with 1) expressing his own thoughts 2) operational tasks expected of an eleven year old as determined by Piaget's model of learning 3) Memory, as illustrated by his scores in vocabulary tests and times tables. Troy's difficulties in school could be secondary to the recent loss of father (died less than a year ago in Vietnam), although unlikely, since his problems are confined to academics and he has never demonstrated any abnormal social interaction with teachers and peers. Would also rule-out dyslexia and drugs.

Troy quickly grew grateful for the label of *slow*, since teachers stopped singling him out and grew to expect very little from him. Even so, Troy continued to struggle in school, remarkable for a child who's IQ would one day register off the charts. Troy wasn't sure what was wrong with him, but he knew he wasn't stupid.

Troy's first insight into his own mental gifts came during a game of handball. The kids in his neighborhood often clustered around the rear brick wall of *Capwell's Department Store*, where a game of handball could always be found. It was a simple game requiring only a wall, a rubber ball, and chalk to mark out the boundaries. Two players would, in turn, hit the ball against the wall with the palm of their hands. For seven year olds, keeping the ball within bounds was mainly by luck; however, Troy could see the physics behind the game. He could see the angles, the momentum, and vectors, and intuitively anticipate the exact location the ball would land after hitting the wall.

At around the same time, Troy picked up a habit he later called *spinning*. He realized he could rotate objects in his mind at will, revealing every angle, every facet. He would sit in the back row during class and spin things—chairs, books, and people. It was a mindless habit, a way to pass time, like doodling or daydreaming. What Troy couldn't yet understand was that this same trick allowed him to see every side of a situation, simultaneously. In a harmless question, he saw problems that the questioner never anticipated. What seemed obvious and simple to the ordinary mind could be frightfully complex to Troy, so much so that he often found himself paralyzed and speechless in front of his teachers.

When the students in Troy's class were asked to memorize and place the fifty states on the map, Troy needed only to look at the map once and simply fill in the map from the picture in his mind. He got a hundred percent and was sent to the principal's office for cheating and then sent home. Leon had beaten him mercilessly until his mother stopped it. He never got another perfect test score again.

The only class Troy enjoyed was art class, the one class where no one was looking over his shoulder, wondering why he was so stupid, or if he was cheating. Not only that, but his art teacher seemed truly interested in Troy's work, even if he didn't quite understand it, as he politely confessed to Troy. Drawing and painting was the perfect outlet for Troy's strange gifts. He drew objects in ways only he could see. When he drew people, he drew all sides and angles at once, as if he were simply unfolding the person

While other twenty-two year olds kids like Leon were off fighting communism ten thousand miles away, Leon was watching it

on TV. Leon had sickle cell disease. During his pain crises, he would lie writhing on the sofa, suffering along with the soldiers on television. A bullet through the gut could not compare with the excruciating pain he felt as the red blood cells in his body sickled and deformed, clogging his blood vessels like thick sludge in a sewage pipe. It even happened in his penis, causing the vessels to engorge, leaving him with a painful erection that could last for days. The only thing that helped was morphine.

Morphine was Leon's life. He used it to keep the pain at bay, but whatever he had to spare, he sold on the street. Leon was a small time dealer, making just enough money to give him a taste of the life he thought he deserved. The only thing that kept him from expanding his little enterprise was the Panthers.

The Panthers ran the neighborhood. They patrolled the streets in Cadillacs, four to a car, heavily armed with shotguns and M1 carbine rifles visible through the rear windows like the turrets of a tank. They disapproved of, but tolerated, Leon's small time dealing so long as his clientele remained exclusively white. On several occasions, they had warned him that if they ever heard of him pedaling his goods to his own people, they would kill him. No questions. No mercy.

Leon stared listlessly at the TV, the sound turned off, watching news clips of wounded marines carried on gurneys, most of them black as far as Leon could tell. The image cut to a clip of Viet Cong soldiers in matching garb, marching in unison, and his thoughts went back to the Panthers and Brother Nathan

The cursed Brother Nathan was their leader, a local celebrity, said to be a personal friend of the late Dr. King, and answered directly to the man himself, Huey Newton. *Little fucker*, Leon thought. *No better than the fuckin' Commies, telling him who he can and can't sell to, trying to prevent a brother from makin' a livin'.*

Troy woke scared. Something had torn him from sleep. He had been dreaming about the woman from the church, the panther woman with the Afro and big breasts. He sat up and listened but heard nothing at first. After a minute of silence passed, he heard the muted crying of a woman followed by the voice of his mother pleading with someone.

Troy hopped out of bed and pressed his face to the keyhole but he could see nothing except that Leon was conspicuously absent from the couch. Slowly, he opened his bedroom door and stepped out into the small living room of their apartment.

A half dozen people filled the apartment's small entrance. Troy spotted Leon pinned against the open door by two large men, his faced sandwiched between one of the man's oversized hands and the barrel of a shotgun. In the far corner of the apartment his mother stood talking with a smallish man. Except for his beret, the little man who stood in the doorway of his apartment looked nothing like the army of giants that filled the living room, all of whom seemed to be watching the little man. He was talking calmly to his mother, who looked anything but calm. She tried to say something through her heavy sobs but the man raised his hand to silence her, not like the way Leon did when he was about to strike you, but slowly and firmly, the way the reverend did at the beginning of his sermons at St. Michael's Church.

The small man turned and nodded to the army of larger men behind him, which parted, revealing a young black girl of no more than fourteen. She wore a man's overcoat and grey baggy sweatpants. She walked barefoot. One eye was swollen shut and the other glassy with tears. The little man reached for her hand and walked her into the apartment and over to where Leon was being held. He whispered something into the girl's ear and girl nodded quickly and turned away and began to cry. As she was led back out of the apartment, the little man turned back to face Leon who was now blubbering, snot dripping from his nose.

Troy watched from the doorway of his room as the men in berets and black leather jackets escorted a frightened whimpering

Leon out of the apartment. This new Leon mesmerized Troy. Leon—whom he had feared from the first moment they met—was, himself, reduced to a frightened sobbing child. Troy ducked quickly into his room.

"Hey, little soldier."

Troy started. It was the little man that had been talking to his mother. Not only did he look nothing like the other men but he dressed nothing like them. He wore horn rimmed glasses and a thick gold necklace worn on the outside of his T-shirt, which was neatly tucked into his grey trousers. *Charlie Never Called Me Nigger!* the shirt read.

"Hey, you don't got to be scared of me, little brother."

Troy now recognized the man. Brother Nathan. It was Brother Nathan that had been talking to his mother in the living room and now stood in his doorway.

"May I come in, young brother?"

Troy nodded.

Brother Nathan nodded and stepped in. He seemed to take the room in and then walked over to Troy's dresser above which Troy had pasted drawings from his art class.

Brother Nathan put his hands behind his back and leaned his face into the drawings for a better look.

"Huh," Brother Nathan kept repeating and for a good two minutes he stood still, hunched over Troy's dresser, looking at the his art work.

"I'll be dammed. Just what I thought," Brother Nathan said, and turned to face Troy. He didn't say anything for a moment. He just seemed to be studying Troy. Finally, Nate's face lit up into a grin.

"Well ain't you a regular Negro Ramanujan."

Troy smiled. He had no idea what Nate was talking about but he sure liked him.

Brother Nathan lay with his hands laced behind his head staring at the constellations of stars that hung an arms-length above him, stars that Nate himself pasted to the plaster ceiling of his flat, while lying on his back on the top bunk bed, like Michelangelo painting the Sistine Chapel. Nate imagined the body of Theseus, his sword raised to slay the half man-half beast. And there was the beautiful Cassiopeia. The stars were actually just tiny glow in the dark peace signs Nathan had bought from a longhaired hippie girl in Berkley. Nate remembered her pretty freckled face, long brown unwashed hair that dipped below her waist and more brown hair sprouting from the cleavage of her armpits.

A cool breeze swept through the open window abutting Nate's bed. From where he lay, Nate had a clear view of the Alameda County Courthouse, a large impressive mass of white marble. The sight of the courthouse always made Nate think about Huey, locked up in San Quentin on charges of kidnapping, assault, and of murder of a police officer.

He had first met Huey Newton at Oakland City College in 1965. Nate had just enrolled while Huey had been an on and off again student for over five years. Already a local celebrity and political activist, Huey divided his time between studying, organizing the local black community, and making a living as a small time hustler and thief.

Like Nate, Huey was a small man but that's where the similarities ended. Huey was handsome, tough and street smart, and no one fucked with him. Nate loved the stories he heard about Huey growing up on the mean streets of the Oakland. When Huey was sixteen, he walked into Bert's, a local pool hall down the block from Berkley High, walked up to biggest man in the room and picked a fight. And then beat the crap out of him.

Huey was hungry for knowledge and recognized Nate's intellect as an asset to himself and the black community, and they spent many hours together discussing politics, philosophy and the future of the black man in America. He was with Huey when Malcolm X was gunned down on February 21st, 1965 and when

Huey and Bobby Seale approached him with the *Ten Points and Platform Program* of the newly formed Panther Party, a list of "what we want and what we believe", Nate was one of the first to sign up. So what if Nate didn't really believe in their methods or their demands? It gave him a chance at what he wanted most in life—a chance to stop being afraid.

And then Nate thoughts made the inevitable turn towards the one memory that would haunt him his entire life, the memory he lay down with every night and woke up to every morning—a bus ride he had taken five years earlier from Washington D.C. to Mississippi.

It was the summer of 1964 and college kids from the East Coast's most prestigious schools played hooky from class in order to lend their support to the Civil Rights Movement by helping blacks in Mississippi register to vote. It was supposed to be a ground roots operation. Students from all over the East Coast would converge at Howard University in Washington, D.C. where they would board ten school buses and make the thousand-mile trip to Mississippi. Once there, they would break up into groups of *twos* and wander the streets of six different cities over seven days, knocking on the doors of homes and local businesses, churches and youth centers, encouraging its black citizens to exercise their right given to them almost a hundred years ago by the Fifteenth Amendment.

They gathered in-between the red brick buildings of Howard University's Tubman Quadrangle—students of all colors and religions—with nothing in common but the privilege of idealism. There was a rally emceed by an interracial couple, and when the rally ended, the students filed into the buses.

Nate took a seat close to the front of the bus next to a pretty, blond Jewish freshman from Georgetown. They had nothing in common. She was white, he was black; she was Jewish, he was Baptist; she was rich, he was poor; but they talked for hours like best friends.

It was dawn when Nate's bus, traveling south on I-55, crossed over from Tennessee into the rural Northeastern Hills of Mississippi. Troy awoke to find the pretty girl from Georgetown no longer next to him. People were talking excitedly. Nate was disoriented but he felt something was wrong. He glanced at his watch. 6:05 AM. Outside the bus window, beautiful thick green trees whizzed by with surprising speed and Nate could feel the bus begin to wobble and swerve.

"They're chasing us!" someone from the back of the bus yelled.

Everyone turned and stared in disbelief at the sight of a half-dozen open bed trucks, overflowing with white men, speeding up the sides of the bus. One of the trucks crawled up on the shoulder, filling the air with a grey dust. It swerved several times toward the side of the bus, trying to get close enough so the men could hit the bus with their bats. For one brief moment Nate was struck with the absurdity of what he was seeing, and an image of the Keystone Cops flashed in his mind, the funny little men crammed into the back of their tiny squad car, swerving back and forth while they brandished their stubby police clubs. And then the image was gone and Nate was just plain scared.

There was a loud crash coming from the rear and the bus began to swerve wildly. His body was flung against the passenger window and the bus lurched to halt on the side of the road. Nate looked out his window just in time to see a coke bottle smack against the window and explode into a cobweb. And then to the amazement of everyone, the bus door swung open and out jumped the driver, and everyone watched in disbelief as the middle-aged white man ran madly into the thicket of woods. Several bottles were launched in his direction as he disappeared into the brush.

After the bus driver abandoned ship, there was tremendous amount of noise—metal hitting glass, metal hitting metal. A young black woman stood up in the front of the bus and began to shout something through a megaphone. There was a loud bang and the rear of the bus filled with smoke, sending a stampede of frightened college kids down the narrow aisle. Nate remembered being carried out of the bus, riding the swell of terrified people. Outside, Nate was thrown to the ground. Dust filled his eyes as he looked around desperately for the young Jewish woman.

A hand gripped his tie, yanking him onto his belly, and as he was being dragged, he found himself fixated on the slivers of dirt underneath the man's long fingernails. Something hard hit Nate in the mouth and he grunted from pain. He rubbed his tongue across his teeth, which felt wet and slimy, and a wave of nausea swept through his gut. Nate looked up at his assailant's mouth where two yellow stained teeth snarled at him through a missing wedge of lip and skin, and in that moment, all the evil in the world came to focus on the man's harelip. Then the twisted mouth spoke.

"I'll be dammed, a monkey in a tie. Now I seen it all."

It was the last thing Nate heard.

Nate awoke in a hospital. Everything from his eyes balls to his chest to his skin hurt. His neck was immobilized in a collar and his right arm hung from the ceiling by a rope pulley. A curtain surrounded his bed and he could hear the voices of the nurses and doctors working on a screaming patient, a black man with a heavy southern accent.

Tears swelled up in Nate's swollen eyes. More than the physical pain, he felt what? Embarrassment? Self–loathing? Anger? No. It was none of those. It was fear. He thought of the man with the harelip grimacing at him like some possessed jack-o-lantern and he felt scared, and then, disgust, for being so weak and naïve. He thought of the pretty Jewish girl sitting next to him and hoped she was okay and felt shame for not being able to protect her. He tried to stop himself from thinking about all the horrible things that could have happened to her and then he began to cry, heavy sobs, that made his ribs feel like they were breaking one by one, all over again. Did he think that a suit and tie would protect him from hatred and stupidity? Didn't they know he was an Ivy man, a Yalie?

Nate never went back to Yale. When they released him from the hospital, he hightailed it back to Oakland where he enrolled in Oakland Community College, and when, three years later, at a Black Panther rally protesting the incarceration of three of their soldiers in front of the Alameda Courthouse, a group of white reporters from the *Oakland Tribune* asked Nate what he was rebelling against, he had been on the verge of answering *Whaddaya got?* like Marlon Brando in *The Wild One*. And would the answer have been that far from the truth? What in the hell was little Nathan Kennedy rebelling against, anyway? Nathan, who had an academic scholarship to Yale University, and was going to be a captain of industry. That was until he'd gotten the shit beat out of him. And then what happened to those ambitions? He had been humiliated. But that was only part of it. Even more than the good life, even more than money and privilege, he wanted never to be scared again, and he wanted the nightmares to end. He thought the Panthers could give him that. And weren't they doing good things? Weren't they in the moral right? He was too afraid to answer his own question.

After he got out of the hospital, he could have just hopped a train back to New Haven and crawled back up into the Ivory Tower and forgotten about the whole fucking thing. Wouldn't that have been the easy road? But of course, he knew the truth, and no amount of rationalizing would change what he knew in his heart. It was fear that led him to where and who he was today. The way a bullied child takes to lifting weights, it was fear that brought him to the Panthers, and not a desire to change the course of the black man in America. And maybe, that was Nate's biggest secret of all. He was where he was not because he believed in what the Panthers were doing, but because he just didn't want to be afraid anymore.

It was three weeks since Leon was taken from the tiny apartment in the Brookfield Village in East Oakland. Troy's mother never mentioned that night and Troy never asked. With each day that Leon stayed away, Troy grew happier while his mother grew increasingly more sullen and indifferent. She was gone often and would not return until after Troy had gone to sleep. She stopped cooking, instead, leaving a few dollars, now and then, on the kitchen table for him to buy groceries.

One unusual afternoon, his mom returned home while the sun was still out and told him to get dressed. Troy asked *why*, but his mom ignored him. He didn't want to leave and demanded to know where his mother was sending him and when she refused, he began to cry.

Troy didn't see the hand that caught him across the cheek. His crying stopped and he just stared at his mother who had clapped both hands over her mouth in horror. He sat down and started to pull on his socks and shoes when the doorbell rang. His mother hadn't moved, still clutching her hands over her mouth, her eyes tearing silently. The doorbell rang again and Troy stood and went to the door and opened it. Two large black men filled the doorway. Each was well over six feet. They wore dark glasses, leather jackets, berets, bandoleers strapped across their broad chests and each clutched matching shotguns. Troy recognized the same two men who had Leon pinned against the wall of their small apartment weeks earlier. Troy puffed out his chest.

"I ain't scared of you," Troy said.

Nate looked like a completely different person. He wore a grey sweatshirt with a large blue Y on the chest and white shorts with green trim and a green four-leaf clover on the right thigh. No beret, leather jacket, boots or any of the other paramilitary trimmings that made up the typical Panther wardrobe. He looked even smaller this time around and his skin lighter. He was changing a record on his player, lowering the needle very carefully onto the spinning vinyl.

Troy sat at on a tattered sofa in Nate's one bedroom apartment. Several copies of the *Amsterdam News* lay on the wooden coffee table, while the floor was littered with stacks of magazines—*MAD Magazine, LIFE,* and *National Geographic.* Small neatly arranged stacks of baseball cards, each held together with crossed rubber bands lay on one of the two kitchen table chairs. An oversized bookshelf was stuffed with books of all shapes and sizes and the walls were plastered with posters of Bruce Lee, Marilyn Monroe, Marlon Brando and The Beatles. Still others showed images of the Panthers, heavily armed in the paramilitary dress, with fists in the air.

The two large men who appeared in Troy's doorway had been sent to make sure Troy made it to his meeting with Nate.

"Sorry for the escorts," Nate said as he welcomed Troy, "but I've known your mom for several years and, well, sometimes she can be a challenge. I wanted to make sure you and I had a chance to talk."

Music blared through a pair of rectangular wooden speakers and Nate fumbled with the volume.

"The Beatles' *White Album.* You like music?"

Troy shrugged.

Nate sat down on the carpet and folded his legs Indian style and seemed to study Troy.

"So, that was pretty scary. I mean, what you saw a few weeks ago…with Leon. How are you and your mama doing?"

Troy shrugged.

"Your mama says you're slow. You got some kind of learning disability. Is that so?"

Troy said nothing.

"Well, is it?" Nate persisted. "Come on, little brother, you can talk. It's just you and me."

Troy considered Nate for a moment.

"Mama talked to a school doctor."

"And?" Nate pushed.

"And that what he says."

To Troy's surprise, Nate laughed, but it was a different kind of laugh than Troy was used to. It was happy and friendly—not cruel—as if he had said something funny.

"Troy, look at me." Troy did.

"Troy, you're no more learning disabled than you are white. And you blackest little bastard I ever seen, excuse my French. Your mama tells me your daddy was killed in Vietnam, one of the first men to go over there."

Troy nodded.

"You miss your daddy?"

Troy shrugged.

"Troy, you ain't gonna get through life shrugging and nodding. When someone asks you a question, you need to answer. And you look them in the eye when you do."

Troy looked Nate in the eye, searching for a sign that Nate was just like all the other grown-ups but he couldn't deny that there was something very different about Nate.

"I didn't know my father that much," Troy answered. And that was the truth. Troy's father unloaded crates of vegetables for a wholesale produce company. All the shipments came in at night, so he slept during the day. But he never hit Troy like Leon, and he didn't smell bad.

"Troy. I'm gonna ask you to play a little game. Close your eyes, young soldier."

Troy hesitated. He could feel the hairs on his neck stand on end and he looked to the door, wondering if the two gorilla-sized men were standing guard just behind it.

"It's okay. I ain't gonna hurt you," Nate said. "Hell, Troy, you're bigger than me."

Troy squinted hard at Nate, and then closed his eyes.

"There's a poster on the wall behind you. Maybe you noticed it when you came in? Can you tell me what it says?"

"It says, 'Charlie never called me...nigger.' Who's Charlie? Is he your friend?"

"Not exactly. That was an easy one. Let's try something a little harder. I saw you looking at my bookshelves. Can you remember the names of any of the books?"

Troy started to turn around and open his eyes.

"Don't open your eyes, and don't turn around. That's the game."

"Which shelf," Troy asked and because his eyes were closed he never did see Nate raise his eyebrows in puzzlement.

"Um, start with the top shelf, Troy."

Nate sat dumbfounded as Troy, one by one, and in order, began reciting the titles as if he were reading them right off the shelf, which was impossible because his eyes were closed, and even if he were peaking, the bookshelf was behind him. There were James McDonald and Ian Fleming mysteries; French novels; political science textbooks left over from college; a King James Bible; an anthology of famous quotations; a collection of Shakespeare's plays; Mao Tse-tung's *Little red*; biographies of Booker T. Washington, Frederick Douglas and Lincoln; Che Guevara's *Guerilla Warfare*; an anthology of Bob Dylan poetry; Robert Williams' *Negroes with Guns; The Little Prince,* and so on.

Troy continued to recite the titles in a one long monotone sentence, occasionally saying the title was not visible on the spine, or the book didn't look like English.

"You can open your eyes now, Troy. Learning disabled, huh?" Nate clapped his hands together, laughed and stood up and slapped Troy on the shoulder.

"Here's the deal, Troy. You're to come here after school every day, and bring your books. I'm gonna help you with your school work. I'm gonna have a little talk with your teachers and your mother, too, just to make sure we're all on the same page. All you have to do is show up and do what I say, and don't get into any trouble at home or school. No strings, Troy. I don't want anything in return."

Nate could see the uncertainty in Troy's eyes.

Troy walked over to where a black felt beret lay in the corner of the apartment and picked it up. He slid it over his head and cocked it smartly to one side and looked at Nate. Nate frowned. It was first time he'd seen Nate look unhappy. Troy knew he had done something wrong.

Nate walked over and gently took the beret off Troy's head and placed both hands on his Troy's shoulders.

"Troy," he said, in a quiet but firm voice. "You are to stay away from the other Panther members. Be polite, but do not listen or believe anything they say."

"But…" Troy began. "But…you're a Panther." Troy shook his head. "I don't get it."

"Troy, when you're my age, the Black Panther Party will be long gone, a small footnote in history. You're different Troy, and you're gonna be so much more than all this." Nate hands made a sweeping gesture over the room, but Troy understood Nate was not talking about the apartment. He didn't know exactly what, but he understood it was big.

In the rear of the bar was an eight-foot billiards table, its green felt worn threadbare and heavily scuffed by stray cues cradled in drunken hands. Subdued and lonely notes from Stan Getz's trumpet could be heard leaking from two old GE speakers mounted behind the bar. It was three in the afternoon and the bar was empty except for Nate, who sat alone at a table in the rear, watching the bar's only other patron, an old man who kept drifting off to sleep. His lips smacked together rhythmically trying to staunch his tongue from slipping between his toothless gums. His arms, which rested on the wooden bar, were skinny with knotted veins and reminded Nate of the naked branches of a Maple tree in the middle of a Connecticut winter. Pulled low over a hairless skull was a black cap festooned with a gold braid that Nate recognized as the official cap of a Pullman Porter.

The Pullman Palace Car Company, built, owned and operated most of the passenger cars from the Civil War to the early half of the 20th century. They set the standards for luxury railway travel and staffed their sleeper cars with polite, articulate Negro men, often taunted for being Uncle Toms. It was not manual labor or factory work, which made it very desirable work, work that was imbued with a certain amount of romance—the chance to travel and even meet celebrities. The man's cap was an older edition, circa 1940s, since replaced with a more modern edition and Nate thought of his father, unwinding after a sixteen-hour workday of cleaning the toilets and making the beds of the sleeper cars.

The men who came to the Sharkey's Bar and Lounge were mostly men from older generations. They were the sorts of men who had problems but did not want to talk about them. Best of all, it was a place you would never find the Panthers. Nate could just relax and not worry about stepping out of character. For a few hours, he could escape the path in life he had chosen.

Nate turned his attention to Abe, the bartender, an enormous man with hands like baseball mitts Nate had heard all the stories about Abe. He had been a professional prizefighter with a bright future. He had even been one of Sonny Liston's favorite sparring partners, but his career was cut short by a seven-year stint in prison for manslaughter.

Some Mafia *gumba* had been pressuring him to throw a fight and he punched the man, a hard right hook that caught him on the temple. The man never saw it coming and died instantly. They said the man had a dent in his head the size off a grapefruit. Abe never said much and never looked anyone in the eye, a habit Troy figured he'd picked up in prison.

And then Nate saw him. He was sitting across from Nate in a booth by himself, hunched over a cup of coffee. He was white, about Nate's age, clean-shaven with short neatly cut brown hair and dressed in a white short-sleeved Izod shirt with khaki slacks. He took a long sip of his coffee and placed a bill under his cup, stood, and began walking towards the rear of the bar where Nate sat.

Nate felt a surge of adrenaline. He scanned the bar for help but of course he was alone, no Panthers, which was why he chose this bar in the first place.

Nate sat up straight, puffed out his meager chest, and watched as the man approached. He could feel his pulse quicken and the familiar fear creep into his gut.

The man stopped directly in front of Nate and smiled.

"Nate, is it really you?"

And then Nate saw it. He was much younger then and his hair hung down to shoulders. He was skinnier too, but the toothy, dimpled grin was the same.

"This is unbelievable," the man said, still smiling, his head shaking from side to side in wonder.

"Chris Brooks," Nate said, more to himself.

"You won't believe this, but I was talking about you just the other day," Chris said. "I was telling someone the bat story. You remember that?"

Nate smiled against his will. He hadn't thought about things like that in years. Nate, Chris Brooks and Todd Hurley were freshman roommates at Yale. Chris had borrowed Tom's lacrosse stick and caught a fruit bat that had gotten into their college residence, Trumbull Hall. Todd poured ketchup all over his neck and clutched it as if trying to staunch the flow of blood and Troy began knocking frantically on this freshman's door, some snot nosed son of a US senator. When the kid opened the door, Todd began screaming that a vampire had bitten him. Then Nate held the door open while Chris released the bat into the kid's room and the three of them pinned the door closed.

The boy almost shit in his pants, banging on the door and screaming to get away from this harmless, vegetarian, flying mammal that was probably more scared than the boy. It had been years since he allowed himself to think about that time of his life. It seemed like someone else's memories.

Chris sat down in front of Nate and looked him over.

"Gosh Nate. How long's it been? Six years?"

"Seven."

"Seven years, huh?"

Chris' face became serious.

"You know, Nate. I was really sad when you didn't come back. I mean, it was a horrible thing what happened to you and the others on that bus." There was a long silence and then Chris' face broke into a big grin.

"Hey," Chris said, slapping Nate's hand playfully. "You remember that night before my microeconomics exam. I was a hair away from a nervous breakdown and you stayed up all night with me, tutoring me. And, voila, I walked out of the test with the second highest grade."

Nate remembered. Chris had got the second highest grade. Nate got the first.

"I remember you wanted to be a lawyer," Nate said. "Or at least your dad wanted you to be one."

Chris smiled and threw his hands up.

"Editor of the Harvard Law Review."

Nate nodded.

"You're a Harvard lawyer, and you spend your leisure time in blue collar dives in all-black neighborhoods. What kind of lawyer does that?" Nate looked hard at Chris.

"A poor one," Chris said with a sheepish grin. "I really am a lawyer. But I work for the government."

Of course, Nate thought. The polo shirt and khakis—clean-cut, clean-shaven—they all looked like they just walked off a tennis court. Yale was a breeding ground for future members of the CIA and FBI. The agencies were constant presences on the campus, along with the nation's biggest banks, consulting and law firms, all looking to sign on the nation's best and brightest.

"Your father must be disappointed," Nate said.

Chris frowned at the mention of his father.

"He was livid. To my father, working for the government is the lowest form of employment, suitable only for the most unambi-tious and lazy." Nate smiled at that, and for a moment, they were both nineteen again, sharing everything, but the moment passed quickly.

"Nate, you got to believe I'm here as your friend. They consider your organization a threat to national security. If it weren't me, it would have been someone else. Jesus, Nate! This wasn't the life you wanted," Chris said, leaning back and making a sweeping gesture over the bar.

"We were roommates, for Christ sakes. I know you, and *this* isn't you. You told me about your father. How he was a Pullman Porter working wretched hours, cleaning up after all the rich, white people. You told me how you were going to be the first black captain of industry. You were going to use your money and clout to better things for your own people. Do you remember? You told me that was the only way to change things. You had to change things from the inside, you would say. And now you're part of a militant organization dedicated to tearing down the very establishment you longed to be a part of. You didn't choose this anymore than you chose what happened to you down in Georgia."

"Mississippi." Nate said.

"Right, Mississippi. I told you not to go. I told you it was dangerous, but you went anyway. You were so idealistic."

Self-pity swelled in Nate's throat.

"Go away, Chris. You shouldn't be here. Things are different. I'm different. You have nothing for me. You can *do* nothing for me. "

"I understand your number's been called."

The self-pity Nate felt was swept away by a surge of anger. *You bastard*, he thought. He wanted to jump up and scream at Chris. But Nate did and said nothing. They weren't friends and hadn't been for years. Nate received his draft card just a couple days earlier and he understood now that the timing was no coincidence.

"I know you, Nate. You're no soldier and you never will be. Not for the Black Panthers, and certainly not for Uncle Sam. You're a pacifist."

No, thought Nate, shamefully. *I'm a coward and the man with the Jack-o-lantern grin laughed and nodded in agreement.*

"I can help you, Nate. I can make it go away. I'm telling you, Nate. Nam is ugly, even uglier than what they show you on TV. I spent some time over there, not in the jungle, but info gathering, and let me tell, you wouldn't survive a week. Of course, we would expect something in turn."

"You want me to be a mole. A snitch. Maybe we meet up here once a week, and I brief you on Panther activities."

Chris leaned back in his chair and raised his hands so his empty palms faced Nate.

"Come on, Nate. You don't believe in that shit anyway. I know that. Hell, our psych-ops people know it, and they're three thousand miles away. Don't look so surprised. We have your whole life on file. We've been watching you for a while now. We need you, Nate. This is your chance to get out of the Panthers and avoid the war. Maybe get your life back on tract. Charlie may never have called you nigger, but he'll sure shoot your ass just the same."

For a fleeting moment, Nate allowed himself to believe the fantasy. Maybe there was a way out of it all, a chance to get back on tract. Maybe go back to school, start his life again. Hell, he was only twenty-five. But it was a fantasy. Too much had happened and there was no going back.

Chris pushed a folded cocktail napkin towards Nate.

"That's my number at the Regency Hotel. I'm leaving tomorrow at ten A.M. Offer expires when I get on the plane." Chris stood and walked around the table and placed his hand on Nate's shoulder.

"You're no fighter, Nate. I know you'll make the right choice. Good to see you, buddy."

He had not told anyone about being drafted. Not the Panthers, not Troy. The truth was, he didn't know what he was going to do.

He considered taking off for Canada or going overseas. He always wanted to backpack through Europe. The only thing he knew for sure was that he would not go to Viet Nam, and he could not go to jail. And then there was Troy. As much as he had grown to love the boy, he could not deny that, deep down, he was jealous, jealous of the life Troy would have, the life Nate wanted for him and would help him get, the life Nate wanted for himself, but that slipped away.

He sat on a brown beanbag in the corner of his bedroom and flipped through a stack of pencil drawings Troy had made for him over the past year, some on quarter-inch ruled paper torn for notebooks, some on colored construction paper from Troy's school art class. Like Ramanujan, the Hindu mathematician who had re-discovered calculus sixty year ago in a small village in the south of India, and was ultimately, himself, discovered by a famous British Mathematician from Trinity College, Troy seemed to have re-discovered the cubism of Picasso. Cubism on speed, is what Nate called it. In his mind, Troy saw his subjects from every possible angle, simultaneously, and literally unfolded his three dimensional subject in his mind with scalpel like precision, and presented it back onto the two dimensional paper. His drawings were kaleidoscopic in their complexity, dizzying in their detail, and mathematical in their precision and symmetry. Usually, the subject—be it a house, person, animal, or tree—was often difficult to recognize.

But where Picasso was offering the world an experiment—a new way of presenting the world through paintings—Nate understood that Troy used his drawings as an outlet for a mind he was still struggling to control. Nate flipped to a crayon drawing he had stared at for many hours, a mosaic of unrecognizable shapes and designs, each housed in tiny rectangles of identical size. Troy had drawn this particular picture on one of their many trips to the Berkley Pier.

At the entrance to the pier was a taco stand and Nate and Troy would pick up a half-dozen fish tacos and two large wax paper cups of tan, milky *orchata*. Ice cold and smelling of almonds and cinna-mon, the drink always reminded Nate of Christmas, a holiday he had not celebrated in many years.

Sitting on the edge of the pier with their legs dangling above the water, they ate their tacos and watched the sailboats and the fisherman. Nate always found comfort siting on the pier. Maybe not as good as being on a boat, or an island in the pacific, but it was an escape nonetheless, as if no longer standing on land meant he had escaped his problems, however briefly.

When they were packing up to leave the pier, Troy had handed Nate the crayon drawing. On the bottom of the picture he had written, *My Friend, Nate*. Some of Troy's drawings were recogniz-able, or at least you could recognize, in the small fragments, clues to its subject—like looking at the scattered pieces of a jigsaw puzzle. But in Troy's portrait of Nate, he could find nothing that resembled a human form, not the wedge of an eye or the curve of a lip—just a confusion of shapes and colors, like shards of a smashed stained-glass window. Nate found the picture disturbing. *Was he so broken, so devoid of any identity that he was unrecognizable, not just to others, but to himself as well? No life, no dreams, and no real purpose?*

But Nate knew he was being ridiculous in projecting his own insecurities and regrets onto Troy's drawing. And besides, he had a purpose, and it was Troy. He had found Troy—discovered him—a true genius, a once in a lifetime mind, and in, of all places, a Black Panther housing project in East Oakland. He would get him out of this shithole. Maybe, he thought, things did happen for a reason and God did have a plan.

"Come on, Troy. We're going for a ride. I wanna talk to you about something."

They left the yellow and cream-colored bungalows of East Bay behind them and headed north past nests of increasingly larger and attractive homes that decorated the hills overlooking San

Francisco Bay. There were no black faces in the passing cars and their white passengers stared suspiciously at Nate and Troy as the green Chevy continued to climb the roads of the Berkley Hills. Nate was relieved he remembered to remove the 12-gauge shotgun from the back seat of the car.

Cross' Point, one mile, the sign read. Cross' Point was a favorite late night hangout spot for the well-to-do high school kids in the surrounding neighborhoods. They would come here to drink, smoke pot, or screw in the back seats of their parent's cars. But in the middle of the day, it was deserted. The rocky ground was scattered with beer cans, cigarette butts, and the occasional condom wrapper.

Nate and Troy got out of the Chevy, hopped over the metal protective railing and made their way onto a large flattened rock. Five yards beyond the rock on which they both sat, the ground dropped off and in the distance was the San Francisco skyline, its geometric skyscrapers etched into a perfectly clear day—blue sky above, blue water below. It was the most magnificent sight Troy had ever seen.

"Amazing, isn't it? Supposed to be one of the five prettiest bays in the world."

And Troy stared at the beautiful city below. *It's like a jewel*, he thought. *A giant, glittering, masterfully cut, ruby.*

"You see it, Troy. I can see you see it—just like I did when I was your age."

For several minutes, Troy and Nate sat in silence, admiring the view, enjoying the quiet. And then Nate spoke.

"You know, my father was a Pullman Porter. You ever heard of them?" Nate asked.

Troy shook his head.

"Yea, well...it was as big deal in those days. The Pullman Porters worked on trains. They were a good looking bunch of black men—well mannered, well spoken, gracious and some even college educated, who had the privilege of cleaning the dirty sheets, fluffing the pillows, cleaning the wash rooms, and preparing the berths for the white travelers of the Southern Pacific Railroad. They were called the world's most perfect servants." Nate laughed at the description.

"It was actually a physically demanding job. The porters didn't sleep much and they were constantly on the go from the moment passengers boarded the train. I remember watching my father demonstrate fixing an upper berth for a new porter. He had to pop the upper berth from the ceiling of the train which took tremendous strength, fasten curtains, arrange the headboards and fix the blankets and pillows. A good porter could do it in three to five minutes—my father could do it in ninety seconds. Doesn't sound too glamorous but in the old days, it was a desired job, and my father was a respected man because of it. Friends and neighbors admired and envied him. When problems or disputes arose in our neighborhood, they were brought to my father who would hand down the final word. He was a trustworthy *negro*—clean, articulate, always dressed in one of the two suites he owned. I guess if white folk could trust him, well then..." Nate shrugged, not finishing his thought.

"My mother would sometimes take my brothers and I to the 16th Street Station in Oakland to see my father. We loved going there—walking into that humongous building with its tall Roman columns and high ceilings, then up the stairs and onto the elevated tracks. Just below were the bay waters, which came right up to the tracts, and across the way was Oakland Hills. I was maybe ten or so. She was very proud of him, my mother. Worshiped him, and he was a good man, never raised his voice, never hit us, and a good provider.

"His train was there when we reached the tracks and my father was already on the deck, walking behind a frail looking white man. The man, crooked and bent from age, walked unsteadily, a cane in each hand, while my father carried two large suite cases. Unlike me, my father was a large, powerful man. He looked striking in his pressed black slacks and white jacket, large nickel buttons and black embroidered cap. People said he looked like Jim Brown." Nate smiled at the comparison.

"All of a sudden, the old white man stumbled, releasing both canes, and he began to sag. My father dropped both suitcases onto their sides and somehow managed to catch the man under his arms just before he went down onto the hard floor.

"My father collected the discarded canes, which he gently gave back to the old man who was still a little dazed, but the old geezer quickly gained his composure and took the canes from my father and turned to look at the suitcases lying on the ground and frowned.

" 'Careless nigger', he spat at my father, and then with surprising speed, he swatted my father twice in the thigh with one cane before spinning and hobbling on toward the station. My father must have seen the horror in my face, and he winked at me and smiled, as if to say he was fine, and then hoisted the suitcases back up in each hand.

"I was angry for days...and embarrassed, but more than anything, I was puzzled as to why my father wasn't."

"Do you miss him?" Troy asked.

"Yea, I do. Although I'm glad he's not around to see me today."

"Why, Nate? He'd be real proud."

Nate looked at Troy and smiled but it was a sad smile.

"You see, Troy, my daddy was from a different generation. In his time, being a Pullman Porter was progress. He would never have approved of the Panthers with their protests, threat of violence and drama. It's not what my father would have wanted for me...and it's not what I want for you."

Nate stared off into the distance.

"You see that skyscraper, Troy."

Troy nodded.

"Somewhere in an office on the top floor of that building is a man working. He sits at a big desk, and every now and then, he looks out the window a mile above the city, and do you know what he sees?"

Troy looked at Nate.

"The same thing you and I are seeing right now," Nate said.

Troy stared from the building, and then to Nate.

"Someday you'll sit in a large office on the top floor of a building just like that one and you look down on the city below and remember sitting here with your friend Nate. Your life isn't here. You got to get out. You got to leave. You don't belong here, Troy. You're better than all this. You have a gift.

"I had dreams once, Troy, that my life was going to be extraordinary, that I would never suffer the indignation that my father had to swallow every day of his working life. It's too late for me ... it's not too late for you. I had my shot, but ... the time wasn't right, the country wasn't ready to let a black man in."

You lie, Chimp! You just a coward! the man spat through the wedge of missing lip. Nate shook the image from his head.

"The Panthers walk the streets with guns, they monitor police violence, organize, educate... but it will be for nothing. America and capitalism is here to stay. Global socialism; Malcolm's nationalism; Kings nonviolence; Che Guevara's revolutionary violence; Mao's pick up the gun BS; Newton's *Ten Point Program*—they will all fail. As they should. There will be no revolution. Change will come from within, slowly, and it will begin with brothers like you... who have the minds and gifts to triumph in the white man's most prestigious institutions."

Nate stared at the skyline, wondering if this were the last time he would ever see it again. He wanted to never forget the way the city looked at this moment. He wished he could burn the image in his mind, the way he knew only Troy could. He wanted every line, angle and shadow, permanently etched into his memory; every color preserved in an image that could never fade, retrievable at will. But he was not Troy.

"I'm leaving, Troy. I'm one-A. You know what that means?"

Troy shook his head.

"I've been drafted, Troy. Uncle Sam wants me to join the army and go fight in Viet Nam. They rejected my conscientious objector status. But I won't go. So...I'm leaving, Troy. Heading to Canada. Maybe Montreal. It's as good a place as any. My French is still pretty good, and well, *Faute de grives, on mange des merles*. Beggars can't be choosers, right?"

"But what's gonna happen to me?" Troy said, his voice starting to quiver.

"That's why we're here, Troy. That's what I want to talk to you about. There's a man I know, a reverend. He's an important man at a very prestigious school in the Northeast. I've talked to him about you. We both think you belong there. It's a place where you will get the attention you deserve and where you'll be challenged. He's waiting for my call as we speak."

Nate put a hand on each of Troy's shoulders.

"Troy, the choice is yours. And you got to choose, right here and right now. You can stay in Oakland with your mother, until the next Leon comes along. You can stay at your school and continue to be misunderstood; your talent and mind wasting away, or you can take advantage of your gift and get an education."

"So, what's it gonna be little soldier?" Nate could see the tears welling up in Troy's eyes.

"Whatever you think, Nate."

"Good, it's settled then." And now Nate felt himself begin to cry and he held out his arms to Nate.

"Now give me a hug, little brother."

PART TWO

1971
CONCORD, NEW HAMPSHIRE

On the third floor of the Academy Building, three hours after the official lights-out, Louis Piedmont and Keith Burns sidestepped cautiously down a vast, grey corridor, the sound of their steps insignificant against the heavy marble floor. Lou led the way, keeping his back close to the far wall, with Keith a breath's distance behind. Lou paused when the stairwell came into view. He raised his fist up high, indicating a stop signal like he'd seen the marines do on TV, then pointed two fingers at his eyes followed by a chopping motion at the stairwell, and finishing with a middle finger table for one solute.

Keith clutched his mouth with a cupped hand in a lame effort to stifle his giggles. Lou punched him on the shoulder and dragged his index finger across his neck. Watching the two boys with stern disapproving looks were several former headmasters elaborately garbed in colorful academic robes. The larger than life portraits showed the men posed with various instruments of learning: a globe, a Latin book, a chemistry beaker and a large wooden paddle. All the men had white hair and wire thin specs and their faces assumed an unwholesome postmortem grey in the scant light.

The Academy Building was the largest building on campus and housed all the non-science classrooms, as well as the Assembly Hall, where the entire school would congregate for various official meetings and the mandatory weekly Wednesday morning assembly. The front of the building wore a large clock that sat on a bell tower overlooking an immaculate groomed lawn, and every morning students would watch the clock nervously as they rushed to their classes, trying to beat the final toll of the bells that announced the beginning and end of each class.

The building was a horseshoe shaped brick structure that enclosed a smaller courtyard where students would lounge between classes, weather permitting. The building had three stories, and from the third floor, one could access several balconies that overlooked the inner courtyard. Many of the almost exclusively male faculty would loiter on the balconies between classes or over their lunch hours, smoking and ogling the few female students that attended the school.

The Academy Building was strictly off limits after lights-out, when all but seniors were required to be in bed, and the boys who crept out of their dormitories and into the old building were committing a serious offense. There were six boys, all from the same dormitory, and the game was called Operation Death. It was really just a variation of tag in which the boy, who was *it*, carried a rolled up sock with the intent of whipping it at the other boys, but of course the real thrill was breaking the rules of their two hundred year old institution.

Twenty minutes passed with no sign of the others, and Lou and Keith dropped their cautious stealth maneuvers for a lazy stroll down the long hallway on the second floor. Keith dragged his hand across the windows as he walked and then stopped abruptly. He got up close to the window and cupped his hands over his eyes and against the glass, as if looking through a pair of binoculars.

"Holy shit!" Keith said, and Lou jogged back over to Keith.

"What the hell?" Lou added. Both boys stood still, their faces pressed up against the window, staring out across the dark courtyard at the opposing wing of the building where another boy stood precariously on the ledge of the third story balcony. It was obvious that he was not one of the other four boys they had snuck out with, obvious mostly because this boy was black.

"He's gonna jump!" Keith said.

"Keep quiet," Lou snapped.

"We gotta do something."

"What are we gonna do, moron? Start banging on the window, screaming *Don't jump!* Then he'd surely jump. Besides, you wanna get caught? Your father would kill you, and then disown you."

At the mention of his father, Keith shut up. Both boys continued to watch, their hearts racing. Then the boy did something neither Lou or Keith would ever forget. He unbuckled his belt, dropped his pants, and began to take a piss onto the courtyard. They stared, flabbergasted, watching the arc of piss disappear into a trickle three stories below.

Troy pulled up his pants and buckled them and sat down on the balcony, allowing his legs to dangle precariously off the edge, three stories high. He never did see the two boys who watched him from the other side of the Academy Building.

How did he get here? Now that he was here, what was he supposed to do? He had so many questions and he wanted so badly to talk to Nate, but he knew it was impossible. Nate was gone and he would never see him again. Troy thought about the Reverend Soki Jones, Nate's friend, the man to whom Nate had passed Troy onto, and his introduction to the Reverend was one of the oddest things he'd ever seen.

As students filed into the giant auditorium through three different entrances for the first Assembly Hall of the new school year, Troy could hear a noise, like rolling thunder, echoing off the walls. It seemed to come from all directions, and as he rode the swell of students into the grand room, the pounding grew louder and faster, its source hidden from Troy, who was unable to see over the heads of the taller upperclassmen who led the way.

Finally, the students began to take their seats and Troy got his first glimpse of the stage where two men of starkly different sizes, stood on either side of a humongous barrel like drum that itself was perched on a four foot tall wood scaffold. The men were naked but for giant diapers fashioned out of white bed sheets. They wore straw sandals and white headbands knotted in the back that displayed the rising sun of the Japanese flag. The man on the left was a small, wiry Asian man with horned rim glasses who Troy later learned was an instructor in the Oriental language department. His partner, banging away at the giant drum in unison, was enormous—well over six feet—with rolls of fat beneath his neck and armpits. His skin was a caramel brown, the color lying somewhere between Troy and the little Asian man.

The two men beat the drum with long sticks using over hand swings in perfect synchrony with each other, each steadily increasing the speed of the beat and force of each swing while sweat dripped down their hairless chests and backs. And then when the noise swelled to a feverish crescendo, the drummers stopped and turned to the audience and bowed, and the sea of students erupted into cheers and howls.

The little man walked off the stage and brought the much larger man a towel and large black robe and after a quick bow, disappeared behind a crimson curtain and Troy turned his attention to the fat man, who now dabbed at his dripping brow and chest before putting on the long robe. The man was even bigger than Troy had first thought, and looked like he must have weighed close to four hundred pounds. His large head wore salt-and-pepper stubble and he had a broad nose, large lips and almond shaped eyes. He looked neither Asian nor black but rather strange concoction of the two.

Stepping up to the front of the stage, the giant man dwarfed the wooden podium that wore the two hundred year old school emblem. He bent over and removed the microphone off the stand and raised a hand the size of a catcher's mitt and the auditorium went silent.

"When will you give up?" he began. A long pause followed, his mammoth head scanning the auditorium, trying to catch the students eyes, or those who dared look away from the weight of his stare.

"I wonder ...when will you give up? And I wonder... if you will remember that moment, years later, looking back on your life. Will you remember that very moment when you gave up your dreams, your hopes... and decided ...to be like everyone else."

Students shifted uncomfortably in their seats.

"Some of you are laughing to yourselves, shaking your heads, thinking to yourselves...'That will never be me. I'll never give up...or settle.'

"Are you so sure?"

And more seats shifted and creaked.

"Will you give up your dreams? Will you abandon the passions that make you unique, and throw up your hands in resignation, and get in line with the rest... or..."

The reverend raised a large finger.

"or... will you risk it all?"

"And when the fear comes, and it will come... it comes to all of us at some point...I ask you...to ask yourself... 'What am I afraid of? What do I have to lose?'"

With sweat still dripping from his brow, the Reverend, or Rev, as he was called, took a drink of water before continuing.

"To believe in something. To devote your life to it. Your industry, your love, your sweat, and to have the courage to pursue it with all your heart. Will your life be your own? Will it be about you, or will you take the easy roads? Will you pack up your dreams for good and join the family business; become a partner in your father's law firm or medical practice? I wonder how many of you will ever know the bliss of believing in something so strongly that you fear not failing...but, rather, never trying."

The Rev scanned the sea of young faces and smiled broadly.

"Does anyone here have the slightest idea of what I'm talking about?"

Students looked around at each other, as if wanting someone else to answer the giant man.

"And if you take that chance, what will you lose?" Rev continued.

"Will you starve? ...Of course not. So what are you afraid of? What will happen if you pursue your dreams? If you fail, will you be any less loved? ...Of course not. If you fail, what do you lose?"

Like the drums, his voice seamed to pick up speed and momentum, bounce of the walls and ceiling.

"But not to try," the mammoth preacher shook his head. "If you don't try, how will you feel forty years from now, when you look back on your lives? Modern medicine tells us the odds are you will live to be old one day, and when you are old, will you remember sitting here today? Will you remember that boy or girl, full of dreams and hopes? Will you remember the moment you gave up and decided to be so... average? This is about your life... my challenge.

"Make your life exceptional...make it unique...make it yours. No," he said, shaking his head.

"On second thought... I wonder...when will you give up?"

Silence, followed by an explosion of cheers and clapping as the entire student body leapt up off their seats. Troy stood with the other students, not wanting to stick out or be the only student not standing. It was Troy's first introduction to the man who would become a four-year fixture in Troy's life.

Reverend Soki Jones stood in the front of Troy, filling the entire doorway of his dorm room.

"So... you're Troy Hunter?" the Rev said.

Troy said nothing. He just studied the man, this funny looking giant.

"You can talk, can't you?" The reverend asked.

Troy nodded.

"Oh, good. I'm so glad they haven't lowered the school's admission standards."

The two said nothing, boy and man just staring at each other as if trying to make sense of the other until the reverend spoke.

"I'm your dorm master... every dormitory has one. My quarters are on the first floor. So we'll be seeing a lot of each other. I'm also the school chaplain and the head instructor in the religion department...so I wear a lot of hats around here. You're a long way from home, Dorothy. Don't think for a second cause you're black that you'll get any special treatment from me. You work hard, don't break the rules, take advantage of the opportunity Nate's given you... in short, don't fuck up."

"Have you heard from Nate?" Troy asked. Rev saw the boy's eyes brighten and he felt sad for the boy.

"No, son, I haven't." He reached out a giant hand and placed it on Troy's shoulder. "I don't expect either of us will. This is your home now, Troy. Welcome."

Unlike his public school in Oakland, the Academy offered nowhere for Troy to hide. His classes were small, each limited to no more than twelve students, all seated around a circular oak table so there was no chance disappearing into the back of a class of fifty kids. The instructors, as they were called, were friendly and seemed to truly love teaching the students which was a far cry from the school teachers he had known back in Oakland. Troy began to realize that there was more to school than just memorizing facts. Here, the students were asked to question the things they learned about; they were mercilessly peppered with questions meant to stir their minds and comments that were intended to provoke heated discussion.

His first class of the year, an introduction to American History, was one he would never forget. The instructor was a tall, muscle bound former marine turned cop turned teacher. He sat at the large round oak table, hands laced in front of him, back ramrod straight, his corduroy sport jacket pullet taught against his deltoids and biceps, looking each student firmly in the eye before talking.

"I'm Sargent John. J. Patterson of the United States Marine Corp, retired."

"Ooora!" the man yelled, startling the class.

"I'm also former Motorcycle Officer John Patterson of the Los Angeles Highway

Patrol."

The man jumped from his seat, swinging one hand to his belt for an imaginary gun and pointing the index finger of the other hand at the class and yelled, "Drop your gun...now!"

Several students almost fell from their seat, the rest breaking out in nervous laughter.

"But you can call me Mr. P." Mr. P said, smiling.

"I've spent half my life carrying a gun...but it was not a gun, but rather history...that saved my life."

"It was history that helped me make sense of the things I've seen and done in my life. I know you don't know what I'm talking about right now, but you will."

Mr. P sat back down and gingerly laced his fingers back together before resting his hands on the table.

"So...was anyone ever in a car accident? The cops show up, right? And what do they do? They question everyone. The people in the cars, the pedestrian walking across the street, the kid on his bicycle, the homeless man sitting on the bench in front of the accident. Each has a story, a version of what really happened, and it's up to the cop to piece together all these different stories and come up with his own version of what happened...right?"

Mr. P continued, not waiting for an answer.

"But the cop has a lot to consider when coming up with his own interpretation of what really happened. He needs to ask himself, was this particular person in the car, or watching from a distance? What stake does the person have in the outcome or does he have any personal interest in who was at fault? Were they injured… did they have insurance…did the observer know one of the people involved in the accident… was the person telling the cop what he saw… blind…or drunk?

"That is history. History is not a series of past events lined up in chronological order. It is living and breathing and constantly evolving. What really happened and why depends on who you ask, where they were when it happened, and their personal interest in the event in question."

Mr. P picked up a large textbook off the table, which sported an American Eagle on its cover and a title that read American History and showed it to the class.

"We will not use a textbook in this class. George Orwell said, 'History is written by the winners.' Maybe history textbooks are… but history is not. So we're going to read the accounts of the not just the winners, but the losers as well. We will read accounts from individuals from all sides and viewpoints, and it will be up to us, to determine what really happened, and why."

Troy sat beneath a large Elm on the edge of the perfectly groomed common grounds and watched the students coming and going from the row of dormitories, massive red brick buildings covered in ivy, its broad leaves giving the illusion from afar that the green turf was growing right up the sides of the buildings. To his left was the Academy building with its cupola bell tower; across from him, the library, a nine story behemoth and the only building that didn't match the rest of the Georgian style red brick buildings; and to his right, the massive grey stone gymnasium which bordered a hundred acres of playing grounds. The air was warm and heavy with the scent of freshly cut grass and Troy breathed in deeply.

"Hey. You're Troy, right?"

Troy looked up to see three boys standing over him. He recognized them from his dorm, and the one called Lou was also in his math class.

"I'm Lou, this in Keith and that's Chauncey."

"What were you doing in the Academy Building last night…" Keith said, before an elbow from Lou silenced him.

"Anyway," Lou continued, flashing Keith a stern look. "Where you from?"

"Oakland," Troy said. "California" he added.

"Yea, we know where Oakland is," Lou said, rolling his eyes at his friends. "Well, anyway…my father…"

"There he goes, thirty seconds into a conversation and he's mentioning his father," the boy called Chauncey said.

"Excuse these two," Lou continued. "They're just jealous. Like I was saying, my father says he talked to the headmaster and he heard you were some kind of genius… or something. That true?"

"Well, if your father said it…must be true," Troy said, which Keith and Chauncey thought was hilarious. Lou glared at his two companions.

"Anyway, since we're in the same dorm and all, you should come hang with us. We could use some brains in our posse. You see what I gotta deal with," Lou said, pointing a thumb over his shoulder at his two buddies. Chauncey shoved Lou who flipped him a bird. The bell tower rang, even measured tolls, signaling the students that it was time for the next class.

"So what do you say?" Lou asked.

"Yea, okay."

"Cool. We'll see you later."

Five boys, all between the ages of fifteen and sixteen, sat on the splintered edge of a wooden pier, their feet dangling over the brackish water of the Boston Harbor as they watched the boats comes and go. The pungent smell of fish was everywhere but it didn't stop Troy from enjoying the morning. He missed the water and looking out over the Boston Harbor made him think of his trips to the San Francisco Bay with Nate. The Harbor was busy this morning with boats of all different shapes and sizes—outreach trawlers coming back from weeklong trips, hunting for scallops; brown wooden sloops with white sails luffing under a strong fall breeze; and the occasional blue and white ferry, shuttling people and cars. Troy's mind wandered back to the present just in time to catch the tail end of a disagreement between Seth and Lou.

"I'm telling you the truth," Seth pleaded.

"You're full of it," Lou said. "Besides, Keith here has something to tell us…a little surprise for all of us. Tell'em Keith."

The four other boys stared at Keith in anticipation.

"Well," Keith said, milking the moment with a dramatic pause. "This guy who goes to M.I.T with my bro' told him about this restaurant in Chinatown where, if you know the right thing to order, they take you upstairs…" Keith stopped and stared at the other boys making sure he had all their undivided attention.

"Then they bring out a dozen really hot Oriental girls and you get to choose any girl you want."

"Whatever," said Chauncey.

"No," Keith said. "It's true. And these Oriental girls…they know things."

"What things?" asked Chauncey.

"Things that American girls don't know. They know ways to please a man. They get special training. It's part of the culture."

"I don't know," Seth said. "Sounds like bullshit to me."

"It's not bullshit," Keith said defensively. "Chinese girls are raised to please their men. They learn from a young age. Haven't you ever her of Geishas?"

"Geishas are Japanese, you moron," said Chauncey.

"Yeah, well you don't have to come if it's such bullshit. You can go back to your dorm room, crawl under your crusty blanket and whack off." Keith pinched his own cheek and began making obscene noises with his mouth.

"So what's the password, the magic phrase?" Troy asked.

Keith smiled smugly before answering.

"Chinese egg rolls."

"That's it?" Lou asked. "Egg rolls?

"No, asshole," Keith snapped. "Not 'egg rolls'....Chinese egg rolls. If you say you want an 'egg roll', you'll get an egg roll. You got to say 'Chinese egg roll.' That's the key."

Lou pulled out a strip of condoms from his backpack and began tearing them off and handing them out to the other boys.

"What's this?" Asked Jerry, a heavyset kid with bad acne and chronic gas.

"What do you think it is?" Lou said. "It's a rubber. You put it on ...unless you want your dick to fall off."

"It can fall off?" said Jerry.

"Maybe you should have given Jerry a tampon instead," said Chauncey.

"Screw you," said Jerry, leaning to his side and lifting his left butt cheek before letting out a loud fart.

"You fucking pig," Chauncey screamed, grabbing his mouth.

It was one of the few Saturdays that the boys didn't have classes, and the five boys, all from the same dormitory, had taken a bus to Boston for the weekend. The plan was to hang out in the city, take in a Red Sox game and then crash some college parties in Cambridge. The visit to Chinatown was not part of the plan, but before they knew what they were doing, the boys had hopped the red line buss to Beach Street where they disembarked in front of a large white stone archway topped by green shingles marking the entry into Chinatown.

"There she is, boys," Keith said. "Beyond that pagoda lay pleasures you can't even imagine."

"That's not a pagoda," Troy said. "It's a *paifang*."

"A what?"

"A *paifong*. A traditional Chinese archway. It's used..." Troy said, then stopped, seeing Keith confused look.

"Forget it," Troy said. "Call it a pagoda for all I care."

"We're about to get laid and Troy's lecturing us about Chinese history," Seth said, swatting Troy on the shoulder.

As the boys passed under the elaborate archway, the scenery underwent an abrupt change in color, smells and sounds. Cryptic Mandarin characters painted gold and red and green; dead, skinned chickens hanging from their necks in store windows like wind-chimes; fish heads, pigs feet, piles of fruits and bushels of funny looking mushrooms, all on display for people to poke, pinch and squeeze. Old men with white hair and long wispy beards sat out front of the shops, smoking funny looking pipes. Music, odd instrumentals, produced from bamboo pipes called qins, along with plucked strings, leaked from apartment windows along with the omnipresent smell of rotten eggs.

The boys followed behind Keith, taking in the sights and sounds, until the group stopped in front of a small unassuming shop called Ma Huang's. A cardboard sign rested on the windowsill showing a mass of squiggles and strokes, and underneath, the English translation, 'Tuday Speshal Barbaku Duk.'

"This it?" Lou asked.

"I think so," Keith answered, although he no longer seemed so sure of himself.

They all looked up to the second story where curtains were drawn shut. Behind those curtains were activities the boys could only begin to imagine. Chauncey let out an audible gulp, and Jerry farted.

It was dark inside the restaurant and they waited for their eyes to adjust before venturing in further. It was even smaller on the inside, with a handful of tables all empty except for one elderly patron sitting against the far wall sipping tea and reading a Chinese paper. A stern looking middle aged Chinese woman, wearing a red embroidered jacket stood in front of a cloudy fishy tank stuffed with sluggish gold fish, their eyes bulging from the sides of their heads and their scales tarnished grey. She waved them over to the one table large enough to accommodate all five of them. None of the boys said anything, all nervous, their mouths dry and their adrenaline pumping.

The woman handed them menus and then returned with small porcelain cups, a pot of tea and a large bowl of fried noodles.

"You order now?" The woman said, flipping open a small notebook and all eyes shifted to Keith, who nodded, puffed out his chest and cleared his throat.

"I... we ," he corrected himself, "would all like to have..." Keith paused, giving his friends one final look, as if to say 'no going back now' and then continued, "Chinese egg rolls."

"OK, five egg roll...what else?" The woman said looking back up from her pad.

The boys stared from Keith to the woman taking their order, their hearts pounding.

"No..no..." Keith said, thinking the waitress must have mis-understood him. "We each want a... Chinese ...egg ...roll," saying each word slowly and deliberately.

"Yeah, yeah. I got it. Six egg roll. That all?"

Keith looked at the woman, her face blank—no wink or nod or half smile to indicate she understood—only a hint of impatience. There was a long uncomfortable silence while the boys looked from Keith to each other before Jerry spoke.

"I could go for some low mien."

"Me too," said Chauncey.

"Do you have pork fried rice?" asked Troy,

"I don't get it," Keith said, watching the waitress disappear into the kitchen through a curtain.

"Maybe he gave you the wrong password," Chauncey offered.

"You suck," said Lou, grabbing a hand full of fried noodles and throwing them at Keith.

"What are we supposed to do with these rubbers," Keith said.

"Why don't you put it on your Chinese egg roll, you dipshit," another suggested.

The boys laughed over the entire lunch, all feeling a certain amount of relief now that the prospect of their first true sexual encounter was gone. They teased Keith, talked about baseball, school and girls. Troy mostly listened. He was not the talker of the group and the other boys understood that and accepted him the way he was.

For Troy, there was nothing quite like a sunny fall day in New England. The air had a crisp bite to it that made a person feel giddy and happy to be alive. It heightened all the senses, and he was convinced that on days like these, he could look farther and hear and smell better. The boys walked for hours soaking in the energy of the city. The Academy, which was their real home, sat tucked away in a sleepy little New England town that would likely not exist without the school, but fortunately, Boston was only a ninety minute bus ride away. In addition to offering big city excitement, Beantown, home to Harvard and M.I.T, was the city where many of the boys expected to spend their college days and the city was full of former Academy graduates.

The boys walked up Brookline Avenue from Kenmore square, carried by the growing crowd, passing men hawking everything from Red Sox hats and pennants to doughy pretzels to miniature Louisville Slugger bats to Italian and Polish sausages grilled over small charcoal fires on the sidewalks.

Hiking up the steep cement steps, they could hear music coming from somewhere within the stadium and then, like a climbing air plane breaking through the clouds, blue sky appeared and as they surfaced high above, they gazed down onto the players warming up on that majestic field. The perfect green diamond, the starch white bases, the virgin red dirt—trimmings on what was arguably the most famous ballpark around. From right field, the deepest in the American league, over the sprawling seats of center field and onto the Green Monster, the left field wall, Troy took in the awesome sight that was Fenway Park.

The National Anthem sung by a beautiful Italian girl followed by the even more melodic cry of 'Play Ball!'; calls from the fans to 'Hit it outta da pahk!', the crack of the bat from the first base hit of the game; the snap of the shortstop's glove around the ball, snatching it off the first bounce and whipping it to the first baseman; the umpire screaming 'Yer outta he-ah!'; the crowd cheering and someone from inside the Red Sox dugout shouting to the umpire 'Whatayu, retahdid?'; the growing chants of 'Red Sox! Red Sox!', louder and louder, until the next batter walked up to the plate and the stadium exploded—'Reh - G, Reh - G' and Reggie Smith digs in for the pitch.

It was 10 PM when the boys finished up outside of what was to be their final destination of the day, the Fly Club, an exclusive all men's club for the chosen few of Harvard University. There were nine such clubs on campus, but the Fly was arguably the most elite, judging by past members, which included an assortment of U.S. Presidents, senators and industry tycoons. Louis Chase Piedmont was their pass into this prestigious institution. Most Harvard students would graduate without ever seeing the inside of the two-hundred-year-old Fly mansion although Troy thought it looked like every other building at Harvard and at the Academy, for that matter.

"Why do we want to go to a party with all guys?" Keith asked, while they were riding the T into Cambridge.

"The club is all guys but they have girls at their parties, moron. And beer, all you can drink," Lou said

"So, are you gonna join the Fly when you get to Harvard?" Troy asked Lou.

Lou shrugged.

"I guess," he said. "All the men in my family did when they were at Harvard."

Lou's family could claim Harvard graduates extending back two hundred years, and his family's name was well known at the school by those in the know. It was a forgone conclusion that when Lou graduated from the Academy, he would attend Harvard, as would twenty percent of his and Troy's Academy classmates. In fact, over half the students graduating the Academy would attend Ivy League schools, and another thirty percent would wind up at other prestigious institutions like MIT, Georgetown, University of Chicago, Stanford, Williams and Amherst. As Troy learned, it was their destiny as Academy graduates to move on to the best colleges.

Over past three years at the Academy, he had grown accustomed if not somewhat numb, to the constant ego boosting that the students received on a daily basis. Centuries before the "everyone is special" movement had taken over the country, the Academy had been telling its students they were not like others—they were special, the chosen few, who were uniquely qualified to be leaders. They were being primed to be the next presidents, senators, or industry tycoons. It was mantra that most of the students ate up and Troy found it bizarre at first, then tiresome and then just plain annoying.

Except for Lou, who was entering his third minute straight of knocking on the oversized front door of the Fly, the boys sat, their backs resting up against the white ionic columns that flanked the marble entry. Over the boys heads hung a flag showing a feline silhouette, poised to strike, a chain slung over her muscular shoulders. Jerry, who had fallen asleep sitting upright, was starting to snore and Keith kicked his foot several times with no effect.

"Maybe no one's home, Lou," Keith said.

"Or maybe they don't want you in their gay club," suggested Chauncey just as the door was swung open by a tall, heavy set white guy of twenty, with thick sandy brown hair. He stared at the group of boys with a blank expression on his face before taking a large swig from his beer stein and wiping the foam from his mouth with the sleeve of his Bruins jersey.

Troy was somewhat taken back by their greeter. With all Lou's hype over this famous old club, he was expecting something with a little more pomp—not necessarily a rolled out red carpet or a bunch of men in multicolored uniforms blowing on bugles—but not a half stoned frat boy.

Music drifted out in the cold night, mixed with voices, male and female, laughing and talking. The older boy continued to stare blankly at his younger guests before finally talking.

"You kids lost?"

"We were invited," answered Lou.

"Yea, sure…go home. It's way after your bedtime."

"Look, we're on the guest list," Lou persisted.

"Oh, well then," the older boy said with an amused smirk on his face. "Let me check the guest list." He took a long swig of the beer and let out a loud belch.

"Sorry, dudes. You ain't on the list."

"I'm Lou Piedmont. My brother is Charles."

He studied Lou for moment and Troy was sure he saw a trace of disdain flicker across the older boy's face.

"You're Charles' little brother? Yea, I see the resemblance. Alright, go on in."

As the boys began to file in, the young man stepped in front of Troy, who took a step back.

"Hold it. He coming too?" the older boy said, staring Troy in the eyes.

"Yea, him too," Lou said, stepping up to the much larger boy who looked from Lou to Troy and then back at Lou. Troy's heart was racing as he waited for someone to make the next move. The older kept looking back and forth between Troy and Lou, considering his options, and after a tense moment, the larger boy shrugged and turned, pushing through the other boys and before disappearing into the house.

"Hey, Troy. Screw that looser," Chauncey said.

"Yea, Troy. That lard-but will be working for you one day. Fuck him," Keith said.

Troy stood in the doorway, his pulse just beginning to slow.

"I'm going for a walk?" Troy said, turning and heading down the marble steps.

"What are you talking about? There are girls up there…older girls!" Keith shouted after him.

"Lay off," Lou said, pushing Keith aside. "Leave 'em be. The man wants to be alone."

The boys stood in the doorway of the Fly watching Troy head across the street, his hands tucked into his jacket pockets.

"Troy," Lou shouted. Troy stopped and turned back to his friends.

"Be cool," Lou said. Troy smiled and waived. He pulled his pea coat tight over his shoulders and headed back towards the Harvard Square T.

Troy took the T back over the Charles River, happy to be out of Cambridge and back into Boston, exiting just across from the Boston Common, the oldest public park in the country. It felt good to be alone and he was grateful for the excuse to slip away without looking like he was just being a downer. Alone time at the Academy was impossible. Believing idle minds led to trouble, life at the Academy was purposely designed to minimize free time, and Troy spent each day running from classes to athletic practices to his on-campus job, and then, back to the dorm for study hours. Even when Troy was not busy, finding time alone when you lived in dormitory full of teenage boys was not likely.

On the edge of the park grounds bordering Tremont Street were clusters of young protesters. It was late and most had discarded their causes along with their makeshift signs and fallen asleep in piles of three and four. Troy navigated through the cardboard signs, which had been scattered along the grass, their hand written protests seemingly devoid of a central theme.

'Hail to the Thief!' and 'Impeach Nixon' 'Yom kippur = War" and 'Fill your hearts, not your gas tanks.' 'Free Charlie!' and 'Free-Byrd!' 'Roe = Murder.' 'No to OPEC' and 'Racism Sucks.'

Further up, a group of Hare Krishnas sat together in a tight circle. They wore matching yellow sheets and shaved skulls with small pony tails sprouting from the back of their heads. Some chanted while others played finger cymbals, but all bounced up and down in unison, completely oblivious to Troy who continued walking, turning left on to Park Street.

Perched at the Corner of Park and Beacon Streets, just across from the State House, Troy found what he was looking for—the Robert Gould Shaw and the Massachusetts 54th Regiment Memorial—a giant bronze relief depicting the first African-American regiment to fight for the Union in the Civil War, and the white colonel who lead them into battle and ultimately to his own death. Troy had read about the soldiers in the classes of Mr. Patterson's, the soldier-turned cop- turned teacher. Details of the massive carving were difficult to discern under a cloudy night sky and he leaned in closer to the memorial for a better look at the soldiers, their youthful faces unmistakably African, with broad flat noses and large full lips. The soldiers all walked while their commander rode high above on his horse.

It was a amazing piece of work, the soldiers so real looking, all marching forward with rifles resting on their shoulders along with their packs and canteens, their faces all different but sharing the same resolute look of purpose and belief. When the Confederate Congress heard that an all-black regiment was preparing to fight against them, they issued a proclamation that the black soldiers who were captured would be tortured and then sold into slavery while their white commander would be executed. Dates, names, cities, battles—any trivial fact associated with the men of the Massachusetts 54th Regiment began to pepper his thoughts—the memory of each fact generating ten more, growing exponentially like a stones hitting the calm flat of a pond, sending out ever expanding rings.

It was like that with Troy. He never forgot anything. As a child, it was a curse but he had learned over the years to control his mind, to catalogue information and access it only when he wanted to—a mental Dewey Decimal System. But every now and then, especially when he was tired, he would lose control, and his mind would begin to bubble over with information.

"Troy", a voice called out from somewhere on the other side of the monument.

A chill ran up Troy's spine at the sound of his name. *Did the voice call out 'boy'?* Troy thought. He looked around but he was alone. He waited for the voice again but nothing followed, just the sound of dried maple leaves pushed along the pavement by a strong breeze.

It was just a trick of his mind—a *pareidolia*—he told himself, remembering the scientific term for this phenomenon. The brain, confronted with an unknown stimulus, tries to make sense of it by matching it to something familiar, like seeing faces in the clouds. But his rationalization did little to suppress his growing fear and he considered moving on, less the voice return.

The sound of a woman crying, this time unmistakable, again coming from behind the monument, startled him.

"Hello?" Troy called out to the voice and the crying immediately stopped.

The monument was fourteen feet high and flanked on either side by a stone wall that was chest high. Troy ran to the northeast wall and hoisted himself up, swinging his legs over before dropping the several feet onto the soft ground below. Troy stood motionless in the dark, the colossal monument shielding him from the meager light that was offered up from the streetlamps on the other side. He heard nothing but his own heavy breathing, and yet, he was aware of another's presence nearby. He could feel it watching him.

He remembered the matchbook he had taken from the Chinatown restaurant, a habit he had learned from Brother Nate, who collected everything and threw away nothing. Troy tore of two matches and lit them and held the small torch towards the base of the monument where a bundled figure sat. His fingers seared with pain as he dropped the matches and sucked on the tips of his thumb and index fingers until the pain subsided.

"Hello," Troy said.

"Over here, honey," answered a hoarse female voice.

He stepped closer and knelt down and lit up two more matches. His heart skipped and his stomach plunged at the sight of his mother, her afro just as big and unruly, her lip busted and one eye swollen shut, just as he had seen so many times before at the hands of Leon.

"Mama," he said, kneeling next to the woman. The smell of urine and feces hit him like a brick and he fought the urge to recoil. She looked up at Troy for the first time and Troy watched as his mother's face began to morph into something unfamiliar and frightening.

"I'll be your mama, baby," the woman said. "You got smack, baby? I'll suck ya dick."

His fingers singed again with pain as he dropped the matches and fell back onto his rear.

The woman began to laugh, a deep throaty sound that quickly deteriorated into a wet hacking cough, and Troy jumped to his feet and took off running away from the monument and deeper into the park. He kept running, his breath labored and his lung screaming for oxygen. He could see the yellow light of several street lamps reflecting off the dark surface of the Duck Pond and just as he reached the cement path that circled the pond, he fell to his knees, gasping for air.

He remained there, knees and palms against the cement, his head down. The contractions of his chest began to slow as the oxygen returned to his body, and then he vomited. He could taste the cheap whiskey that he and the boys had passed around during the ball game. It had burned on the way down but now, mixed with bile and stomach acid, it burned twice as much on the way back up.

When he was sure he was done vomiting, he rolled on his side, bringing his legs up to his stomach and wrapping his arms around his knees. Troy began to cry. They were his first tears since he left home over three years ago and he didn't try to stop them.

Nine months ago, he stopped receiving letters from his mother. He had tried calling her from the Rev's apartment but the number had been disconnected. More months passed without word from his mother. One Sunday night, Reverend Jones knocked on Troy's door thirty minutes after official lights out. He was shirtless, which not unusual, and although he was still a mammoth of a man and filled the doorway, Troy noticed he had lost weight. Skin, pleated with stretch marks, sagged around his waist. He seemed more tired these days and looked to have aged overnight.

The Rev pulled out the wooden desk chair and turned it to face Troy, who sat up on the side of his bed, his eyes still adjusting to the light. The chair creaked under the weight of the Rev.

"I need to talk with you, Troy. It's about your mama."

Troy nodded but said nothing.

"We don't know where she is," said the Rev. "When was the last letter you got from her?"

Troy shrugged again, not looking at the Rev, his attention fixed to a spot on the wooden floor.

"You still writing to her?" asked the Rev, but Troy didn't respond. "Troy? Son...I'm talking to you."

Troy reached over to the small nightstand next to his twin bed and pulled out a stack of letters and handed them to Rev who flipped through the thick stack. They were all unopened and all bore a red stamp—*Return to sender*. They were all addressed to Troy's mom in Oakland. Rev handed them back to Troy.

"Is she dead?" Troy asked, speaking now for the first time. The Rev let out a large sigh.

"I don't know, Troy. I suppose it's possible," the Rev said. "Troy, you're still a boy. If for no other reason than legal, you need a guardian. Someone who can make the decisions for you that you aren't old enough to make. Someone to look after your best interests. I'd like to be that for you. If it's okay with you."

Troy shrugged. He liked the Rev well enough.

The Rev nodded and stood. He seemed poised to leave but remained standing in the doorway before turning back to face Troy.

"You know, son, your mother was never your responsibility. You're exactly where you're mother wanted you to be, and whether she told you or not, she was always proud of you." Rev closed the door behind him.

Troy was now officially a ward of the school, and he thought of Nate, who had warned Troy that this day would come.

"Your mother loves you, little brother," Nate told him, looking out over the San Francisco Bay. "That doesn't mean she knows what's best for you. Parents are supposed to... but they're just human. And your mom...well, she's had a rough life...your father dying in the war, an all. She's makes bad decisions 'cause she don't know anything else."

Troy didn't like it when Nate talked about his mother but he listened.

"Day's gonna come, Troy, when you gonna be tempted to abandon your life, drop what you're doing, discard your responsibilities... and run to her. You're gonna feel the guilt. It's gonna twist your stomach into knots and play games with your mind. But you can't save her, Troy. It ain't your job. You got to be strong, Troy. You got to be strong."

Lying in the park, Troy thought of Nate's warning. He told himself it was the guilt toying with his mind, conjuring up the image of his mother and superimposing it on a homeless skid. Guilt over having abandoned his mother to the Leons of the world. Guilt that he got out, and she didn't.

You got to be strong. Get up little soldier.

He pushed himself up and dusted his clothes off and continued walking. Ten minutes later, he surfaced from the park onto Tremont Street and continued towards the source of noise and light that drifted from one block over. Another few minutes and night turned to day as the meager light from the tall streetlamps were over powered by multicolored blinking bulbs clustered into all sorts of shapes—giant arrows, triple XXXs, big red lips, pussy cats and curvy feminine figures—all blinking and winking at passers-by. Groups of men walked down the narrow sidewalks, weaving back and forth from intoxication and giddiness. Cars rolled slowly down the streets, bumper-to-bumper, and every now and then, hookers would run out onto the street and surround a car, like a cluster pigeons fighting over a crust of bread. The girls would bang on car roofs, reach in through the driver's windows and grab the driver's crotch, and rub their bare bottoms and breasts against windshields.

Troy knew this was the Combat Zone, the official red light district of the city and homes to places with names like *Two o' Clock Club*, *Good Time Charlie*, *I Naked* and *Teddy Bear Lounge*. He read the signs as he walked—performers with cool names like Princess Cheyenne, Panama Red, Evan Miles and the Creamers, and of course, the hip saxophone of Roger Pace. He started to feel better, enjoying the cool night, the anonymity, and the comfort of strangers.

Troy needed to pee but was pretty sure none of these establishments would let a teenager in to use the *John*, and he turned down a narrow cobble stone street in search of a secluded spot to do his business. The longer he walked, the darker it grew. Light dripping from windows several stories up filtered through the metal fire escapes, casting menacing shadows, like prison bars onto the brick walls on either side of Troy and he was beginning to have second thoughts when he heard someone cry out.

'Oww," screamed a man. "You fuckin' bitch," followed by a grunt, this time from a woman.

Troy searched the ground for stick, a rock, anything that he could use as a weapon. He picked up a glass bottle but dropped it in favor of a metal tube with a handle on one end, the kind used to pull a children's little red wagon.

More cries from the woman. Troy ran full speed further down the alley almost colliding into the large man who was now shouting.

"You nigger whore!"

The man had his pants down around his ankles, exposing a pale hairy ass which he violently thrust into the dark of a recessed doorway. His left arm was extended forward, his fist clutching what Troy realized was a woman's afro. The memory of finding Leon on top of his mother the first time he walked in on the two of them popped into his head. He cocked the metal tube back like Reggie Smith. This time he was ready.

"Get off her," Troy said, startling the man, who hopped back exposing the woman's naked bottom. He reached down and pulled up his pants, fumbling with the zipper. He was an enormous man, as big as the Rev, with a bushy thick beard and mustache and an American flag bandana around his head. He looked like one of those bikers, the Hells Angels, who cruised around Oakland on their loud motorcycles, snarling at everyone who looked their way.

"You little fucker," the man said, regaining his composure now that he had his pants up. His eyes were wide with fury and he lunged for Troy who swung the metal tubing at the same instant catching the man square in the knee. The man screamed and tumbled forward.

"My fuckin' knee. You bastard. You fuckin' broke my knee," the man howled. Troy cocked the pipe back and stepped in closer for another swing. The biker rolled his body into Troy, catching the hem of Troy's pants, and yanked hard, flipping Troy onto his back, sending the metal tube tumbling from his hands. With surprising speed for a large man, he mounted Troy and shot off a right hand that caught Troy just above his left eye sending his head bouncing off the pavement. Troy saw the man reach behind him and then the glimmer of steel in the man's hand.

He's gonna shoot me, thought Troy, and in the same instant that the small revolver was leveled at his face, the gun was knocked from the man's hand. Troy became aware of other people around him and watched as several pairs of hands grabbed the biker by his leather jacket and dragged him off.

Troy lay on his back, dazed, looking up at the large clouds visible through a strip of night sky wedged between the tops of the buildings. They lumbered over the rooftops, slow and steady, like legless grey elephants. He thought of a TV show he had seen about jellyfish that live deep under the ocean, iridescent blue creatures with glass exoskeletons, floating weightless in water so dark and still, it could have been outer space.

The torso of a man, upside down, filled Troy's line of sight. The man stepped over Troy, who still lay flat on his back, and knelt down next to him. He was black, with a mustache and long lamb chop sideburns sticking out from a white broad rimmed fur hat. He reached out with one finger and poked Troy above the left eye, which caused Troy to grunt from the pain.

"Ain't broken. You'll live," the man said, standing back up, giving Troy a good look at the man's matching fur coat, before the fur garbed man turned his attention back to the burly, bearded biker who was being held against the wall by two others.

"My knee," the man moaned.

"Mothafucka, you isn't gonna have to worry 'bout your knee no *mo'*, said the man in the fur coat and hat. "You want to beat and rape the ladies—you stick to the snow and lay of the kinky tops. You dig me, man?"

"Fuck you eggplant," the biker spat.

Troy, still on the hard cobble stones, saw nothing, but heard the thud, like a hammer smashing a pumpkin and a grunt from the biker followed by silence.

"Whoa, Marv. Nice shot. Whada you wanna us to do with him?"

"Get rid of the rapin' piece of shit. *Fo'* good. Aint no one gonna fuck with my traps."

The man in the long fur coat turned back to face the young woman who had pulled her shorts back up and was sitting in the doorway, rubbing her lip which was swelling fast.

"And jus' whadafuck you think you doin'?" the man, who was called Marvin, asked. "Turn your ass out onto the street and fo' what? So you can leave your ho' stroll, come down here fo' free-lance work."

"Pimp stick this bitch, Marvin," said another man.

"Yo, be still!" Marvin snapped. "Don't interrupt me when I'm schoolin'."

"Sorry Marv."

"Now look at you…and you wus gonna be my bottom bitch…"

"Marvin, I swear, baby…" the woman squeaked.

"Shut up," Marvin snapped and Troy could hear the familiar sound of skin slapping skin.

"Leave her alone," Troy said, pushing himself up as the alley and everything in it began to spin. He could feel his left eye starting to swell shut and he wondered how he was going to explain this to the Rev, although at the moment, it seemed the least of his concerns.

"Damm, Marv. You gonna let that boy talk to you that way?"

"Shut it!" Marvin snapped. "Clean that bitch up. I'll deal with her later."

"And the boy?" asked one of Marvin's goons, a fat sweaty man who also wore a white fedora, only his wasn't made of fur.

Marvin knelt down again in front of Troy.

"You brave, little brotha. Stupid… but brave." Marvin said. "Take him inside."

Troy watched ribbons of smoke curl up towards the ceiling fans like genies coaxed from their bottles as the woman on stage twisted and contorted her body, reminding Troy of the buttered, doughy pretzels he and his friends bought from a vendor at the ball park. She was topless, and under different circumstances, and had both eyes been working, and his head not throbbing, he might have been more excited about the show. He thought of his friends at the Fly Club and doubted they were getting a show as good as this, but then again, they probably hadn't had the crap beat out of them or had a gun shoved in their faces, either.

Troy sat in the rear of the club in an oversized circular booth of white plastic beset with small black and red fluffy pillows of different shapes—diamonds, spades, clubs and hearts. Everything in the club seemed to be covered in either red velvet or mirrors. The air was stale and sour, and he was grateful for the cigarette smoke, which seemed to lessen the more offensive smell of sweat, vomit and beer that threatened to overwhelm him. Across from him sat one of Marvin's heavy-set sidekicks whom he remembered from out in the alley. The man was smoking a joint and swaying to the music and every time the dancer would twist into a new and unnatural position, he would put the joint between his lips and clap and nod appreciatively.

Marvin appeared and slid into the booth next to his buddy and across from Troy. Gone was the white fur coat and hat. He wore a cream colored button-down silk shirt splattered with pink spots and he pinched the material near the stains and vigorously rubbed a wet cloth over them, growing more and more frustrated.

"Fuck, I thought you said club soda would work?" Marvin complained.

"It's supposed to get out blood stains," his fat friend said. "I read it somewhere."

"Like you can read, you fat mothafucka. Aw, hell," Marvin said, tossing the wet cloth onto the table. He peeled off his shirt and studied the stains before rolling the shirt into a ball and dropping it onto the floor.

Troy kept his one good eye on Marvin. He was not as big a man as he first thought, but he looked strong, with ropey biceps and a chiseled chest that was covered with scars as thick as leaches. Tattooed on his right shoulder, in Latin, to Troy's surprise, were the words PATER, PECCAVI

"Pater peccavi," Troy read out load. "Father, forgive me."

Marvin looked from Troy then back to his fat buddy who eyes were growing increasingly blood-shot.

"Would you check out this smart little mothafucka!" Marvin said.

"All the students at my school are required to study Latin," Troy said, shrugging. "And Greek."

"No shit? Sounds like a fuckin' waste," Marvin said. "*Pater, peccavi* is the beginning of a Catholic confession. Father, forgive me, for I have sinned…"

"I know what is," Troy said, and then went on to recite from memory, "*Pater, peccavi in caelum et coram te, et iam non sum dignus vocari filius tuus*. But why do you have it on your shoulder?"

"It means what it say," Marvin said, his voice sounding annoyed. "It means the *Man* up there," Marvin said, pointing to the ceiling where a fan made from faux palm leaves spun, "should forgive me my sins. It means I done bad things."

"You still do bad things," Troy said. Marvin stared at him, his face showing neither anger nor amusement.

"I've known brothers like you," Troy ventured on, and Marvin's right arm flew up from under the table with blinding speed, the silver blade of a stiletto snapping open before coming to rest beneath the angle of Troy's jaw.

"Boy, you don't know nothin' 'bout me," Marvin said in a quiet voice that frightened Troy more than anything else that night. "What…you think 'cause I saved your black ass from that hillbilly that I won't cut your heart out without thinkin' twice?"

"You really want to know what this means," he asked, removing the blade from Troy's neck and pointing the tip to his tattooed deltoid.

"It means…I'm a bad man. I know it and God know it…and I ain't ever gonna change. That why it stays here, on me," he said, again taping the blade on his shoulder. "Saves me the time of going to confession."

Marvin sat back and folded the knife closed just as a waitress appeared. She placed two cans of Schlitz on the table. Marvin grabbed one and popped the top and pushed it in front of Troy.

"Have a drink. You look like you need it," Marvin said, opening the other can and taking a long swig.

For a moment, Troy studied the bull on the beer can and then took a drink.

"You watch movies?" Marvin asked.

Troy nodded.

"It's like Eddie says in *Superfly*. You seen it? Best fuckin' movie ever. 'It's a rotten game …but it's the only one the *Man* left us to play.'

"You said it, boss," the fat man said raising his own beer.

"Rev says that's bullshit," Troy said, not believing the words that just left his mouth and bracing himself for the mean end of Marvin's knife, but it never came.

"Rev? Who's that?" a more subdued Marvin asked.

"The Reverend. Of our school. Reverend Jones."

"Sounds like a smart cat."

"He is. He says blaming things on the Man is a cop-out, an excuse for laziness and that everyone is responsible for themselves."

Marvin didn't respond and the waitress appeared again, this time dropping a plate in front of Troy on which sat a raw two inch thick marbled rib-eye. Troy eyed the steak suspiciously and pushed the plate back away.

"I'm not hungry," he said.

"It ain't for your stomach," Marvin said, grabbing the frigid slab of beef and slapping it into Troy's hand, then pushing them both up to Troy's swollen face.

"What the hell you doin' in the Combat Zone anyway, boy?" Marvin asked. "Lookin' to lose your virginity…maybe catch the bad blood in the exchange. Shit," Marvin said, shaking his head back and forth. "Your parents know what you up to?"

"Don't got any," Troy said, the large steak still covering most his face.

"Yea, me neither. You lookin' for sympathy, you in the wrong place. So where you live if you ain't got no family?"

"I live at my school."

"Well, that sucks."

Troy shrugged.

"It's not so bad," Troy said. "I live in a dormitory with a bunch of other boys but I got my own room."

"Mm, sounds queer. So where is this school? What's it called?"

"The Academy. 'Bout an hour north."

"Yea, I heard of it. I thought that place was just for rich white kids."

"That's what everyone says, but it's not like that. I got some good friends there. The teachers are nice."

"Yea, well. Good for you then. You want one of those for your belly?" Marvin asked Troy, who took the steak from his eye.

"I'm not hungry. How's my eye look?" Troy asked, letting the steak down.

Marvin shook his head and pushed Troy's hand along with the steak back onto the swollen eye.

"Looked better with the steak on."

"You home, Troy," said an unfamiliar voice and a hand gently shook his shoulder.

Troy slowly opened his right eye, his left stayed shut, swollen and aching. He lay on his side, his legs curled up to his chest and his face pressed again the furry white back seat of a Cadillac El Dorado. He pushed himself up and swung his legs onto the floor. His head throbbed both from the beating he'd taken and his stomach churned. He burped and the taste of three-hour old beer made him want to vomit all over again. Sitting across from him, wearing a Boston Celtic's sweatshirt, was Marvin. He was hatless, exposing a badly receding hairline and he wore a pair of reading glasses which made him look much older than the man Troy first met a few hours earlier.

The car was stopped on Main Street, which ran through the middle of the Academy campus, separating the dormitories and gymnasium from the academic and administrative buildings. As expected, the campus was deserted at four in the morning.

"You know, I got me a son 'bout your age…but his momma don't let me see him. I send them money, she send me pictures," Marvin said, looking out the window over at the top of his reading glasses at the illuminated tower of the Academy Building, the face of the clock glowing high above like a full moon.

"Thanks," Troy said, sticking out his hand for Marvin, who looked at it, slightly amused, and then smiled and shook Troy's hand.

"Yo, Troy!" Marvin said, just as Troy was about to push the door shut. Troy leaned down and stuck his head back into the large cabin of the Cadillac. Marvin was again looking out his window.

"Things happen for a reason. You here, in the place, for a reason," he said. "You special, Troy. I can tell. You gonna do great things one day. I know it."

Troy waited for Marvin to face him but he just kept staring out his window and after a minute passed in silence, Troy closed the door and watched as the long white El Dorado drove off.

Ten minutes later, Troy was lying in his own bed, sound asleep and dreaming that he was a boy again, running to St. Michael's Church for breakfast before the doors to the church closed.

It was graduation week at the Academy and the campus was a madhouse of visitors from as close as Boston and as far as Tibet. Luxury cars and more than a few chauffeured limousines were squeezed in behind dormitories, in front of the gymnasium, and along the neighboring towns' narrow streets. The Academy offered a host of activities for parents and family which were spread out over four days and would culminate in Sunday's graduation ceremony, which was to be held outside on the lawn in front of the Academy Building, rain or shine.

The school shelled out big money each year for the festivities, partly as a final justification for the high tuition that parents dropped on their kid's education and partly as investment meant to keep the donations rolling in so that the Academy could maintain an endowment that rivaled most big universities. The largest chunk of money was spent on the commencement speaker, as there was nothing more impressive to parents than having a former US president or Nobel Prize laureate give the final farewell address to their children.

While Troy's friends begrudgingly played host to their visiting families, Troy was a hundred miles away and even farther in his mind. He sat in the same chair he had sat in for the past eight Saturdays, half reading and half watching the Reverend Jones sleep. With each passing week, the man who had become the closest thing he had to family was growing unrecognizable. Once the largest man he had ever met, the Reverend now weighed less than Troy. His eyes were sunken deep into their sockets and his skin was jaundiced and hung slack over his cheekbones. His teeth had all been pulled out, a procedure meant to reduce his risk of infection while he underwent the chemotherapy which robbed him of his hair and what little appetite he had left.

A vase full of sunflowers sat next to his hospital bed. Behind the Reverend was a mosaic of get-well cards taped to wall by the nurses, most sent from Academy students, former and current, and Troy recognized the handwriting of more than a few of his own classmates. One of the cards, dated from a few months back, read, "Rev, if you don't make it, can I have your apartment! Miss your cooking! Lou!" It was written before everyone knew just how sick the Rev was, and Troy was sure Lou wished he could have taken the card back. Second to Troy, who visited every weekend, Lou was the student who visited the Rev most.

"Still here?" the Reverend said, his once powerfully distinctive voice now hoarse and unrecognizable.

Troy closed his book and smiled.

"I was just looking at all your get-well cards."

"Yes, I'm very popular," Rev smiled, his dry, cracked lips parting just enough to give Troy a glimpse of his toothless pink gums.

"What are we reading?"

Troy flashed Rev the cover of his novel, Conrad's *Heart of Darkness*.

"How many times have you read that?"

Troy shrugged.

"I know why I would re-read a book that I've particularly enjoyed, but why in the name of God would you ever re-read anything, since I know you could recite anything you read by memory after the first read? "

Troy didn't answer at first and the Rev thought maybe he was just ignoring the question as he often did when he was uncomfortable.

"I don't know," Troy finally answered. "Why listen to a song if you already know the lyrics by heart? Reciting the book in my head from memory is not the same as reading it."

"I guess that makes sense," the Rev said, looking out the window of his small private room on the eighth floor of the Massachusetts General Hospital.

"Looks like rain," Rev said. "I want to go outside."

"You know you can't. The doctors said the risk for infection is too high."

"Doctors!" the Rev scoffed. "God forbid, I catch an infection and die before the doctors have a chance to slowly poison me. I've haven't been outside in months. I just want to get out of here."

Tears began to collect in the deep sockets of the Rev's sunken eyes.

"I don't want to do this anymore. I don't want to do this anymore."

Reverend Jones tried to push himself up into a sitting position but the strength wasn't there and he settled for tugging at the white sheets that covered his torso until they fell to the floor exposing his cannibalized body. Neck, chest, abdomen, arm and groin all spouted clear tubes that carried fluids, some clear and others muddy colored, to or from the Rev's body, Troy couldn't tell. Troy jumped to his feet just as the monitor, hanging from the ceiling, began to chirp and blink, and, as if taking cue, the Rev's breathing grew labored and his lips turned blue.

Even before Troy could shout for help, two nurses burst into the room shoving Troy aside as they attended to the reverend. One pulled the clear tubing from his nose and exchanged it for a full-face mask which she plugged into a tank of oxygen on the wall, while the other injected something into one of the IV lines that pierced the reverend's jugular vein. Within seconds, the reverends breathing slowed and color returned to his face, all which seemed to satisfy the machines on the wall, which immediately ceased their chirps and beeps.

"He'll be okay," said one of the nurses, covering the reverend back up.

"But he'll be out for a while if you want to come back later."

Troy thanked the nurses but said he would stay. He looked out the window as the first drops of rain began to fall. The outbursts were becoming more frequent and unpredictable. One minute the Rev was lucid and calm and the next, he was shouting and fighting to unplug himself from the wires and tubes, which seemed to slowly overgrow him like the ivy that grew unchecked over the brick walls of the Academy's buildings.

Troy pulled his chair closer to the Rev's hospital bed, slid off his shoes and rested his feet on the edge of the Rev's mattress. Troy's feet sunk into the bed, which was fitted with a special air filled mattress meant to reduce the risk for bedsores. He closed his eyes and waited a few minutes to see if sleep would find him, but as tired as he was, sleep was not in the forecast.

He opened his eyes and watched the Rev, now snoring peacefully beneath the plastic face mask. The previous Saturday, sitting in the same seat as he sat now, Troy listened as the reverend shared his funeral plans with Troy. It was only a matter of days now, the doctors had told Troy. The Rev knew it as well and he didn't need a doctor to tell him. The cancer, which started in his pancreas, was now everywhere, and Troy had come to accept that for the third time in his eighteen years, he would lose a father, and with that knowledge came guilt that he had been a bad son to this man who selflessly took him under his wing.

In a matter of fact tone, Rev explained to Troy the arrangements he had made. He was going to be cremated. Half of his ashes would be sent to Hawaii where the Reverend still had family. The other half would be placed in an urn and remain at the Academy Church where a small service would be held for the students and faculty.

As wealthy as the Academy was, the board of trustees couldn't justify creating a separate religion and philosophy department like you would find at a college or university. Instead, and to the Rev's chagrin, they combined the two disciplines under one department, which the Reverend Jones presided over as Chairman of the Department of Religion and Philosophy. Maybe as compensation for being given the anathema task of trying to meld of two disciplines that weren't meant to be melded, rational belief and blind faith, the Rev was awarded one hour each week to preside over a non-denominational sermon of his own creation, to be given at the Academy Church each Wednesday evening.

Officially, the Academy Church claimed no one religion over another, and on the massive wooden doors, engraved onto a bronze plate are the words 'A non-denominational house of worship.' Once inside, it had all the trappings of a typical New England Episcopalian Church, complete with altar, pulpit, pews, flower stands and credence tables, all of which explained the ellipsis that followed their claim of non-denomination, a frank omission that the words on the front doors did not tell the whole story.

The Rev's sermons were optional for students and faculty and open to the public as well, and for the first three years of his time at the Academy, Troy attended faithfully, understanding that how important these Wednesday evenings were for the Rev. They were an outlet for his personal beliefs, a way to continue his true calling of spreading the word of Jesus, even if he was prohibited from mentioning the savior by name, and so when Troy stopped going during his senior year, the Rev was understandably hurt even if he didn't actually say as much.

Maybe because he felt bad for missing his Rev's Wednesday sermons, Troy started a new tradition of showing up unannounced to some of the Rev's intro classes to philosophy and religion, classes designed for the younger classmen, and for a while, it seemed to lift the Rev's spirits. The younger classmen seemed to enjoy it as well, delighting in the back and forth banter between the Reverend and Troy, whose genius made him somewhat of minor celebrity among the younger students.

As a student in these very same classes a few years earlier, Troy was brilliant if not unoriginal. Absorbing the ideas of world's greatest thinkers with ease, Troy played with their ideas as if they were the crude tools of a caveman. At times, he was amused at the weakness of the arguments; Troy did not have to punch holes in them himself, but merely choose another of history greatest thinkers who already did the work for him. With every theory put forth by some brilliant mind from history, Troy would just dip into his bottomless memory and counter with an equally persuasive argument to the opposite, thought up by someone else, thus saving him the trouble. It was like a giant game of tic-tac toe that never ends and can't be won.

Troy dazzled, and his instructors cooed with approval, all except the Rev, who harbored his own fears. He worried that this exponential growth of knowledge was plunging Troy into nihilistic depression, a Socratic dilemma of sorts in which the more Troy knew, the less he felt knew, and the less he cared to know.

One fall day, Troy made an unannounced visit to one of the Rev's intro classes on philosophy. He took a seat in the rear of the class, the rest of the students gathered around the wooden table along with the Rev, who nodded and winked at Troy.

"It's one thing to argue the existence of a higher power by pointing to the physical world. The world, like a complicated watch, needs a maker, and so on, but there are some who would argue the existence of a higher power by looking at our actions as humans. Our capacity for goodness. Our ability to differentiate right from wrong. Is everyone familiar with the *golden rule*?"

"Do unto others as you would have them do unto you," a young lady responded.

"Right. Jesus from the Book of Mathew. The Torah says love you neighbor as would yourself. Two thousand years before Jesus, the Egyptians, in there code of law, *The Maat*, commands, 'Do to the doer to cause that he do to you.' How 'bout Mohamhad? He said 'Hurt no one so that no one may hurt you.' And Buddha said 'Putting oneself in the place of another, one should not kill nor cause another to kill.' The same concept but from different peoples scattered about the globes, and uttered during different millenniums.

"Could a shared innate sense of right and wrong be a coincidence?" the Rev asked. When no one spoke up, Troy took his cue.

"Maybe the golden rule is nothing more the axiom of Darwinism, a necessity for survival, built into the genetic code of all humans," Troy said from behind the rear of the class. "For any society to survive and propagate, the *golden rule* must be followed."

The Rev's eyebrows arched and he eyed his students.

"Well, is he right? Is the *golden rule* just something built into our genes? Something instinctual."

"But not everyone follows the *golden rule*. If it was in our genetics, I would think more people would follow than not," answered the same young girl.

"Another way to frame the question is, is belief in a higher power necessary to live as a good person, or do we possess a moral compass independent of any higher power?"

"Maybe belief in God is written in our genetic code, too," another student chimed in.

"But not everyone believes in God. What about atheists?" a third student added.

"What are you defining as atheist?" Troy Chimed in. "Hindu doesn't believe in Christ, does that make him an atheist? To a Christian who believes in Christ as the savior, is a Muslim any different from an atheist?"

Rev mopped his brow and smiled.

"Wow, looks like things just got even more complicated. Anyone want to answer Troy?"

"Well, the Muslim, Hindu and Christians all accept the existence of a higher power, whereas the atheist doesn't."

"By denying the existence of a higher power, does the atheist not elevate the human to a higher standard of moral responsibility?" asked Troy.

The Rev smiled.

"You're talking about self-respect. The argument that the need for a higher power somehow deprives humans of dignity. Without a moral law passed down from a superior being, man would live in chaos. Man needs the carrot of afterlife waived in front of him in order to motivate man to act morally. Does the belief in an afterlife sully the value of this life?"

Troy shrugged.

"Maybe it does. What religion doesn't have a death wish, a belief that the end will come and their god will appear, and those who are believers will be separated from the non-believer and the believer will take this rightful place next to god... or maybe get his forty virgins, or whatever. If that's not demeaning, what is? I have studied history and the people who made it."

"As have I," said the Rev.

"Yes," said Troy. "And one thing's clear... the majority of atrocities in the world are committed by believers rather than unbelievers."

Troy felt horrible the moment he said it. The bell tower tolled, and the students, who typically reacted to the bell with Pavlovian predictability, by grabbing their books and high-tailing it out the door, remained in their seats, waiting for the Rev's response, but none came.

"That's all for today, class," the Rev said, never taking his eyes off Troy.

The Rev frowned, and Troy realized he had gone too far. This was an intro class to philosophy, and he was there to help the Rev stimulate lively discussion, not antagonize the Rev, but for a brief moment, he didn't care. Troy was angry, but about what, he couldn't be sure. Troy wondered if he was acting out, or rebelling against the person most resembling a parent, hitting the reverend where he knew it would hurt the most. Maybe that was part of it. The anger, gone as quick as it came, left Troy feeling ashamed.

"You know, son. I don't care what these students believe in. Jesus, Buddha, Mohamed, the tooth fairy... just so long as they believe in something."

Troy nodded and as hard as it was, he maintained eye contact with the Rev.

"I realize I can't see the world like you do, Troy. I don't know what it's like to have your gift, or the difficulties that come with having a mind like yours, but you need to find something to believe in, even if you have to invent it. Truth is whatever you choose to believe. Decide what you believe in, Troy and then give in to it. Don't fight or question it."

Troy looked down.

"Don't look away, son. Never look away. Dou you understand, Troy?"

"Troy?"

Troy looked up to find the Rev awake again.

"How are you feeling?"

'Better. What happened? Did I flip out again?"

"Sort of."

The Rev tried to feign a laugh. He pulled the oxygen mask off and Troy stood and helped him replace it with the less cumbersome nasal cannula.

"Thank you," the Rev said. "That's much better. A horrible way to spend a Saturday, isn't it? You know, Troy, I watched my mother die. I sat in front of her and watched her…just like you're sitting there watching me. Worst time of my life. I loved her but I hated being there, having to watch her cling to her last few moments while one organ after another failed. And of course, I felt guilty for feeling like I did…for wanting her to… go… quicker."

Troy didn't respond. One of the monitors that regulated the IV medication being pumped into the reverend began to beep and Troy walked over and played with the tubing, untangling the lines as best he could until the beeping stopped.

"That's the first time you've ever mentioned your mother," Troy said. "I asked you once but you said 'Another day.' Maybe today's that day? If you feel strong enough."

"Well, I don't suppose I'll feel stronger tomorrow," the Reverend said. "My mother was Japanese, which you knew. She was sixteen years old and working as a prostitute in a little brothel on Hotel Street in Honolulu. Her name was Hiroko. From what my mother told me, my father was a southern boy from Georgia who served in the US Navy as a mess attendant on the USS Arizona. He was a negro, as was the popular term back then.

"I don't need to tell you what happened to the USS Arizona but as my mother would tell me years later, dying in a small hospital room that makes this one look like the a suite at the Four Seasons, I was conceived on December 6th, 1941. Just another Saturday night and my father was one of my mother's regulars which I suppose I should be grateful for, or my mother may have never even known his name or that he had died in the attack on Pearl Harbor.

"The brothel she worked at was one of the few that allowed negro servicemen, although, they were required to use a separate entrance through the back and there were only a handful of girls that the negro sailors could choose from, all of who had some type of physical deformity. One had a harelip, another was missing an arm, and my mother was born with a club foot. She was born in Tokyo, into a wealthy family but was given up my her mother to escape the Japanese practice of *Mabiki* in which unwanted or deformed babies were murdered by wrapping rice paper over their mouths. Her mother gave her to her uncle, a man disgraced for something—I never found out—who was sailing for Hawaii but the uncle didn't survive the boat ride over."

Rev began to cough and Troy stood quickly but the Rev shook his head and waived Troy off.

"I'm okay. Could you give me sip of water?" he asked, and Troy poured water from a glass pitcher. He held the glass near Rev's face and threaded the straw between his cracked lips.

"Thank you," he said, and continued talking.

"In 1942, President Roosevelt signed an Executive Order ..." the Rev stopped in mid thought and scratched his head before turning to Troy.

"9066," said Troy.

"Yes...thanks... Executive Order 9066 declaring all people of Japanese ancestry, potential security threats, and my mother, eight and a half months pregnant with me, was thrown onto a ship and sent to the mainland and placed in an internment camp in California.

"Manzana, the camp where I was born and would live for the next three years, was the first home I ever knew. Instead of picket fences we had bobbed-wire that circled the compound, which was funny 'cause there was nothing but desert for a hundred miles in every direction. We all lived in identical barracks, which were lined up in neat rows and within our barrack, my mother and I shared a room to ourselves, which was actually just a twelve by twelve square foot area with curtains for walls.

"I made friends, played and went to school, and when the war ended, we moved to San Francisco where my mother continued the only profession she knew and would continue until her heart failed.

"I was about your age when she died. The doctor's said it was heart failure from syphilis...occupational hazard. They put her in an oxygen tent and gave her penicillin. She wasted away before my eyes. Years later, I reconnected with a childhood friend from my Manzana days—Abe Tanaka. He's now a doctor at UCLA, a big-shot heart specialist, and I told him about my mother. He said something was not quite right about the story and he did some investigating. He thinks she was misdiagnosed and never had syphilis. Thought she has something called Takayasu's, a rare autoimmune disease that attacks your blood vessels. She might have survived had they made the right diagnosis, but ..."

The reverend closed his eyes and Troy thought he might fall back to sleep but then he spoke.

"I'm sorry, Troy," Rev said, his eyes still closed.

"Sorry? For what?"

"For leaving you. You must be getting tired of people letting you down."

The reverend opened his eyes and studied Troy's face, the young man's expression blank and inscrutable as always.

"You don't need to worry 'bout me." Troy said. "I'll be fine."

"I know you will. In few days, you'll graduate and then it's off to New Haven

where you will attend the greatest American university. I'm very proud of you. I wish

I could have left you more. Had I known I would be given a son so late in life I would

have been better prepared. I would've saved more. Taken better care of myself."

"You've done plenty for me. I don't need anything... and I have my

Scholarship," Troy said.

"Scholarships only pay for so much. You need money to live, to buy food and clothes...and have some fun."

"Stop worrying. I'll be fine."

"Yes, I've never doubted that. But...this will help," the reverend said, nodding to the nightstand where an envelope rested up against the vase stuffed with sunflowers.

"Open it," Rev said.

Troy reached for envelope and gave Rev a puzzled look as he unfolded the letter.

It was a letter from a Boston law firm, and monogrammed at the top of the page in gold leaf were the names—*Carter, Reese and Rabinowitz, Attorneys At Law.*

Dear Reverend Soki Jones,

We are contacting you as the legal guardian of Troy Hunter. Our law firm has been retained to execute a trust fund that has been created for the benefit of Troy Hunter. As part of the stipulation of the trust fund, the benefactor of this trust has asked to remain anonymous. Please contact our office to discuss the details. A bank account in Troy Hunter's name will need to be set up so that Mr. Hunter may begin to receive his monthly stipends.

Sincerely,

Abe Rabinowitz, Esq.

"Anonymous?" Troy asked.

"Yes. It seems you have a secret fan. I've passed this on to a friend of mine who is also my attorney. He'll help you. I've written his name and number on the back of the letter."

"What if I don't want it?"

"Don't be an idiot. You're to receive a thousand dollars on the fifteenth of each month, the remainder to be distributed in one lump sum when you turn twenty five."

"Remainder? How much would be left?"

The Reverend smiled.

88

"Call the number on the back of the letter."

Troy folded the letter and tucked it back into the envelope. The rain picked up and both Troy and the Rev stared out the window as the drops battered the glass, grateful for the distraction

"I worry about you, Troy," the Rev said. "You're restless, son."

Troy didn't respond.

"Look at me, son. So…Do you know who might have given you such a generous gift?"

"No," he said. "I have no idea." Troy looked back at the window where the rain was now coming down hard. Nate, Troy thought. Who else could it be?

The law offices of Carter, Reese, and Rabinowitz sat on the 36th floor of One Boston Place, a steel skyscraper that dwarfed the other buildings of Boston's financial district like a big brother. Troy approached the receptionist who was safely tucked behind several feet of polished granite. He smiled and nodded and placed an envelope in front of her. After casting Troy a dubious look, she returned his smile and reached for letter, keeping it at arms distance as she opened it.

"Oh, yes, Mr. Hunter. Mr. Rabinowitz is expecting you. Please, have a seat and he'll be right with you.

The waiting room, a cavernous affair of a marble and oak, was empty but for two older silver haired men in dark blue suits seated next to each other. The monochromatic duos kept their noses buried in their newspapers as Troy chose a seat next to a window offering an impressive view of the harbor curling under the Zakim Bridge.

"Mr. Hunter, Mr. Rabinowitz can see you now."

Troy was led down a wide marble hallway past several glass-walled conference rooms and into the corner office of Abe Rabinowitz, one of the three founding partner of the law firm. Abe leaned back in his chair and talked into the phone. Unlike the formality and heaviness of the waiting room, Abe's office was sleek and streamlined like the façade of One Boston Place, most of the furniture constructed of glass and steel with a few black Napa leather sofas thrown in.

Abe smiled and waved a stubby finger at one of the three chairs in front of his desk. He covered the mouthpiece of the phone.

"Hon', can you bring us a couple of Cokes," Abe said to the young woman who walked Troy from the waiting room and then winked at Troy as if the two of them had just shared an inside joke.

"Alright, buddy. I gotta go. I got a client here. We'll talk, okay... okay...all right. Goodbye." Abe hung up the phone and sighed.

He looked at Troy.

"What a *meshuggah*. You know, crazy?" Abe spun his finger around one ear as if still not sure Troy understood.

Troy figured Abe for mid-fifties. An afro of kinky orange hair framed a round cherubic face covered in freckles the color of coffee stains. His compact body was squeezed into a blue suit and his silk gold tie matched the handkerchief peeking out of his jacket pocket.

"So, Mr. Hunter, I hear you just graduated from the Academy. Wow. That's fantastic. Wish my kids had that kind of motivation." Abe frowned at a silver picture frame, one of the many perched on Abe's sizeable desk.

"Your family must be very proud. So, let's get to it. What we have here is a mandatory trust, which means we, as the employed trustee, have no discretion over the principle sum or income to be distributed. On the other hand, we have been entrusted to invest the principle sum as we see fit. So, instead of the principle sitting in the bank, earning a couple of percent a year, we will invest it for you in a moderately aggressive fund with the idea of getting you anywhere from seven to ten percent a year return. Of course we take a percentage of the profits and we charge a fee which comes out of the principle. Although your principle will increase—we hope," Abe laughed, "your monthly stipend as outlined by your benefactor remains the same. When you reach the age of twenty-five, the remaining principle is turned over to you."

"Who is the benefactor?"

Abe frowned.

"The benefactor is to remain anonymous. I thought you understood that."

"Anonymous until when? Until I'm twenty-five?"

Abe scratched his head and said "Well, I suppose indefinitely, if that is the benefactor's choice."

"How can I find out who's doing this?"

"Well, you can't. That's part of the reason firms like ours are hired. We're entrusted to protect the identity of the source."

Abe pushed his chair back and opened his palms as if inviting Troy closer for a hug.

"Hey, it's cool. You're golden, man. You're going to receive seven hundred dollars a month, tax free, for the next eight years, all for doing nothing. You should be celebrating, man. You hit the jackpot. And then when you're twenty-five, the remainder of the principle is turned over to you."

"How much is that?"

Abe shook his head.

"Uh-uh. Can't divulge that either. Part of the stipulation of the trust. So, did you have bank account set up? I just need the bank name and account number and we'll get things rolling."

Troy handed Abe his bank ledger showing twenty-five dollars, the minimal amount he needed to open a checking account.

"Excellent. I'll also need some emergency contacts."

Troy shook his head and Abe frowned.

"Mother or father? Siblings?"

Troy looked out the window. It was an impressive view and he wondered how Mr. Rabinowitz got much done with the whole city competing for his attention.

"There must be someone that you keep in touch with? I mean, a nice kid like you? With everything you got going for you?"

Troy stood and Abe flinched. It was a subtle movement, an unconscious reflex, but he had seen it too many times not to notice. He walked to the window and looked down on to the Boston Common. He wondered if Nate was out there, maybe staring up at him.

"How 'bout this Soki Jones? Do you want to use him as your emergency contact?"

"He's dead."

Abe shook his head a clasped his hands together.

"Kid, you have anybody lookin' out for you?"

Obviously, Mr. Rabinowitz or I wouldn't be standing in your office right now, Troy thought, but said nothing. Where are you, Nate?

PART THREE

1985
MONTRÉAL, QUEBEC, CANADA

With headlights off, a lone taxi idled on the corner of *rue St-Jaques* and *Saint-Urbain*, just across from *Le Place d'Armes* Hotel in Old Montréal. Its driver sat comfortably behind the wheel, sipping from a small tin mug filled with strong Turkish coffee and reading yesterday's *La Presse*. Although the on-duty light, which sat atop the yellow Chevy Malibu had been turned off, the driver kept the engine running and the heater on high. It was early November and the temperature had dipped into the teens, cold even by Québec standards.

It was a favorite spot for him to park his cab, offering a magnificent view of the twin gothic towers of the *Baslique Notre Dame de Montréal*. In addition, one never knew when a good fare might come along, as there were several pricey hotels nearby, all of which kept taxis in high demand.

More of a home than the one-bedroom apartment he rented, his cab had become a warm, safe womb, made even more comfortable by various accessories accumulated over the past decade: a Chicago Bears neck cushion someone had left in the back seat; a spill proof coffee mug with a non-slip bottom; an electric seat warmer that plugged into his car lighter; and a stack of a books that kept him company when business was slow.

It had taken years, but the cab driver had finally reached a place in life where he could call himself happy. Of course, he had his own thoughts about happiness; thoughts that even he would acknowledge were, in some way, shaped by a lifetime of disappointments. Happiness, he believed, was directly related to the amount of control one had over one's own life, and he had come to appreciate that the smaller the square footage, the greater likelihood of achieving happiness. As luck would have it, the cabin of his taxicab was just the right size.

But lately, something had changed. A sense of unease had pushed its way into his universe, disrupting an equanimity that had taken years to achieve. At first, he couldn't put his finger on it. It was a just a feeling of sorts, not quite a feeling of impending doom, but certainly a foreboding. It was the sense that things just weren't right, like that most familiar sensation of walking into a room and knowing that something has been moved but you just can't figure out what.

After several days living with the odd feeling, he realized what it was he was picking up on. It was a feeling he had not felt in many years.

I'm being watched, he thought.

Rationally, he knew it made no sense. For the past two decades, he lived the life of a loner and he couldn't think of a single person who had any sort of vested interest in whether he lived or died. Outside of his taxi, he avoided people, the depths of his relationships with other humans measured by the fare meter on his dashboard. It was his job to ferry people to and from their lives, all the while choosing not to participate in the whole game. He was truly disengaged.

A knock on his window startled the driver, sending a mouthful of coffee onto his pants.

Realizing he had frightened the cabbie, the man stepped back. The driver stared at the man for several moments. He took him for late fifties, well dressed with silver hair and tortoise shell glasses. He was bundled up in a kaki Burberry overcoat, cinched at the waste. A red patterned scarf cradled his chin, the color matching his nose and cheeks, which glowed from a frigid evening breeze.

The cab driver's eyes traveled to a glint of metal at the man's wrist where a steel and gold Rolex peaked out between his coat sleeve and leather glove. *A good fare*, the cabbie thought. He flipped the on-duty light on, popped open the trunk and waived the man over.

The man smiled and nodded. He threw his bag into the trunk and plopped himself down in the back seat with a sigh of relief.

"*Merci*," the man said.

"*Tu vas oú?*" *Where to?* the cabbie asked, watching the man through the rear view mirror.

"*Je veux aller au l'aéroport.*" *The airport.*

"*Très bien.*"

The man blew into his hands and rubbed them together, and said "*Il fait froid. Je déteste voyager en hiver.*" *It's cold. I hate traveling in the winter.*

"*L'automne.*" *Fall*

"*Comment?*" *Pardon?*

"*Il fait l'automme.*" *It's Fall*, the cabbie corrected.

"*Ah...C'est vrai.*" *Ah ... that's true.*

"*Pardon...Parlez-vous anglais?*" *Excuse me, but do you speak English?*

"*Oui.*"

"You're American," the passenger said and smiled. "You're French is very good. But it's not Canadian French...it's Parisian. You lived in France?"

"No. I studied in school."

The man nodded.

"Well, thanks for picking me up. It looked like you were on your break. It's just so dam cold. I thought I'd take a walk before heading to the airport, but after few minutes, I couldn't feel my face."

The cabbie smiled politely into the rear view mirror.

"Couldn't help noticing all your books," the passenger said, peaking over the front seat. "Sartre, Turgenev, Singer. That's some heavy reading."

The driver glanced at the passenger seat, covered in used paperbacks.

"I think I have some Stephen King and John Grisham in there as well. Makes the time pass faster."

"Ah. I see. You're only passing through."

The cabbie glanced at his passenger through the rear view mirror.

"How's that?"

"Oh, nothing. It's just that most people our age complain about running out of time. You're trying speed it up. I'm Jerry, by the way."

The cabbie frowned, and nodded towards the paper license taped to his dashboard.

The passenger leaned forward and pushed his glasses onto the bridge of his nose.

"Nathaniel Kennedy," the man read.

"Nate," the cabbie said.

"Well, it's good to meet a fellow landsman. So, what brought you to Montreal? Certainly not the weather. I'll bet it was a woman. It's always a woman."

The passenger chuckled.

Nate knew the man was just being friendly. Whenever he picked up a talkative American, the question was bound to come up, and even though the Vietnam War was a distant memory for most, the question caused him terrible anxiety, especially when there was the remote possibility that the passenger had served in Nam.

Nate's answer had always been 'school.' He came over to study, he would say, and wound up staying. That usually satisfied most queries.

But for some reason, Nate didn't want to lie as he had so many times over the years. For the first time, the idea of lying seemed exhausting. Maybe it had something to do with the way he was feeling over the past week, he thought

"The war," Nate answered, shocked to hear the truth slip from his own lips. "I didn't want to go to Viet Nam. So, I moved to Canada."

The man seemed to think about that for a moment.

"Well,' the man said in a thoughtful tone. "As someone who did two tours in Nam, I can't say I blame you. Besides, you came out on the right side of history, am I right? So, do you get back to the states much?"

Nate shook his head, and said, "Not since the day I left."

"Well, why the hell not? You do know that Carter pardoned all draft dodgers in '77?"

Nate cringed at the phrase 'draft dodger,' not that it wasn't an accurate description of what he was, but he had not heard the phrase uttered out loud in so long.

"Well, let me you tell you, Nate. The country's changed. No one cares. It's ancient history, my friend."

"Dorval International Airport," Nate said as they turned into the airport entrance. "What airline?"

"United," the passenger said. "Well, it's good to meet you, Nate. I didn't mean pick at an old scab but you really should think about getting back to the states."

Nate looked at the passenger through the mirror. The man seemed sincere.

"Thanks," Nate said. "But there's nothing there for me."

"How can that be? I'm sure there are plenty of people who missed you when you left."

"Maybe then. But now? I don't think there's a single person in the states that would be happy by my sudden appearance. Here we are. United." Nate threw the car into park and popped the trunk. The passenger hopped out and grabbed his bag and walked back up to the driver's side and leaned down into Nate's open window.

"What's the damage?"

"Thirty-eight dollars even," Nate said, and then added, "Canadian dollars."

"There you are," the passenger said, handing Nate a skinny envelope.

"What's this?" Nate asked.

"It's a letter, Nate. What, you don't have letters here in Canada? Take care, Nate."

Nate watched as the man disappeared through a pair of automatic sliding glass door and into the crowd of travelers.

Troy flipped through the photographs, not liking what he saw. Nate had aged poorly. His small frame had accumulated a lot of weight, and his baldhead had grown a crown of grey hairs that connected to a full mustache and beard, equally gray. Thinking back, it occurred to Troy that Nate shaving his head while the rest of the Panthers grew out their Afros was less a statement of individualism rather than an attempt to hide premature baldness. The wire-rimmed glasses remained the same.

Like a black Kris Kringle, thought Troy.

Looking at the photos of his old friend, it was painfully clear to Troy that Nate had become a very lonely man. Other than the clerk at a convenience store or a passenger in his cab, there were no photos showing Troy interacting with anyone in any fashion that suggested a familiarity. He had only wanted Nate found and the letter delivered, but the investigator he hired threw in some photographs free of charge.

Troy stuck the photos back into their envelope and pushed it aside in favor of another, similar envelope. He stared at it for several minutes before emptying its contents onto the table.

The top page was a poor quality photocopy of a passport. He could make out the words *Republika NG Pilipinas*, and beneath, a headshot of a clean-shaven Asian man. There were several more photocopies of various legal documents: an expired work visa with Manila listed as the issuing post; several student visas, also expired; a Massachusetts driver's license; and a green card, all featuring the same young man whose name was Arturo Manuel Bautista.

Troy discarded the documents in favor of Arturo's senior yearbook page, photocopied from Harvard's Class of '79 yearbook. Mr. Bautista had delicate, almost feminine features and his hair was cut short in contrast to the style of the time. The blurb adjacent to his photograph claimed that he had graduated Phi Beta Kappa with a double major in political science and chemistry; he played squash and was editor of the Lampoon, Harvard's underground satirical magazine. As a teenager, Troy had spent many lazy Sunday afternoons in the Lampoon castle with his friends from the Academy, eating pizza and reading through old editions of the Harvard Lampoon.

Someone fussed with the lock to his front door and Troy put down the photos and listened. A minute later, the tinkering stopped and was followed by the sound of a fist pounding on the door.

"Open the fuck up!"

Troy turned the bolts of the three locks.

"This key you gave me doesn't work," Louis said, handing Troy an aluminum key as he made a beeline for the kitchen.

Troy examined the key and frowned.

"That's 'cause this isn't my key. Don't tell me you lost it?"

He could hear Lou digging around in the refrigerator.

"Jesus, Troy. Don't you have anything to drink?"

"They're going to charge me for the key, plus the cost of replacing the locks if you've lost it."

Lou popped his head out from the kitchen and stared at Troy in disbelief.

"There you go again with the money. You're not livin' in the Oakland projects anymore. You make a lot of money, Troy. I'm afraid to open your pantry. I might find hundreds of those little packets of ketchup and mustard swiped from all those fast food joints you eat at. You haven't changed a bit. You're still just like when I first met you, wrapping up your leftovers in paper napkins as if you weren't sure when you were gonna see food again."

"Just find my key."

Lou disappeared back into the kitchen and emerged a minute later holding a can of generic orange soda.

"You cheap fuck. You can't even buy brand name soda." Lou took a sip and wrinkled his nose.

"Disgusting," he said, and then stared at Troy.

"Dude, you're not even dressed. We got to be there in thirty minutes."

Lou wedged open the venetians blinds on the sole window of Troy's modest kitchen and stared down at the New York Harbor where the Staten Island Ferry, painted a harsh municipal orange, just docked.

"Who the fuck lives in the Battery?"

"I like the view," Troy called out from his bedroom. "Besides, I could have walked. The theater is not too far from here."

Lou looked out to Liberty Island where Lady Liberty stood, modestly concealed, beneath a steel scaffolding, while workers raced to fix her up in preparation for her upcoming centennial celebration.

"Yeah, well, it was the old man's idea to send a driver. Probably afraid we were gonna miss his gay-ass play."

"Who'd he send?"

"The Jew."

The Jew was Ira, a former *Mossad* agent who looked more like a mild mannered physics professor than a deadly killer. The old man, who went by many names including, the master puppeteer, liked to hire foreign paramilitary types and had a slew of foreign drivers and bodyguards. Lou called them the United Nations of Psychopathic Killers.

Lou and Troy slipped into back seat of a black Lincoln town car.

"Good evening, Mister Hunter," Ira said through a small window that separated the driver from the Town Car's oversized cabin.

"Hello, Ira. Sorry I'm late."

"It's no problem, Mister Hunter."

"Hey Ira," Lou said. "Did you hear the one about the Jew, the nigger and the Episcopalian?"

Ira was silent, his eye's flickering between the road, Lou and Troy. Troy and Lou exchanged nervous glances, growing increasingly more uncomfortable with each passing second of silence.

Ira broke into a laugh and both Troy and Lou sighed with relief.

"Yes, I get. It is us, right? The three of us. That's very good, Louis."

The theater was packed and there was still twenty minutes to curtain call. The guests mingled while snacking on artfully rolled bites of sushi served from ceramic boats toted by young women dressed as alabaster faced geishas. An old Japanese man walked amongst the guests, taking requests for origami, his knobby fingers folding squares of paper into animals with mind-blowing speed. Several women stood in line waiting to have their faces painted like Kabuki masks.

"What a circus," Lou said.

Troy had been in the theater once before and it looked like the old man had sunk a lot of money into the restoration. The entry stairwell, previously just a narrow wooden staircase, was now a four lane highway of alabaster stone rises with polished granite tread. A fourteen-foot high ceiling of Venetian plaster had been fitted with fiber optic lights giving guests the feeling that they were walking up to the gates of heaven under a starlit sky. Separating the stairwell and the theater were a pair of circa 1930s Edgar Brandt nickel doors which the old man had shipped over from Paris. The walls of the theater—burred walnut with ebony and nickel accents—were covered in lambskin in a diamond pattern and the seats re-upholstered in plush velvet.

It was here that Troy had first met the old man and the meeting was as odd as any he had ever participated in. The theater had changed a lot since that first meeting, but then again, so had Troy's impression of the old man. In a flip-flop worthy of Dorian Gray, the theater had blossomed into a magnificent work of architecture while the old man had decayed, at least in Troy's eyes.

Troy had heard the old man described in so many different ways, it was hard to believe people were talking about just one man. Compassionate, fierce, disarming, avuncular, inspiring, benevolent, shrewd. One employee had referred to him as a philosopher-king. Another described him a human gyroscope, a man who always managed to land on his feet no matter what situation he was thrown into.

As to how Troy wound up working for the old man, it was hard to say. Yes, there was something magnetic about him. He had possessed that intangible quality that so many great men of history are said to have possessed—a trait that inspired followers. But Troy knew it was more than that. The truth, when Troy was honest with himself, was that when he first met the old man, he thought that, just maybe, he had found a new father, that paternal figure that he seemed fated to lose over and over. He thought again of their first meeting two years ago.

Theater Alley, buried in the rear end of Manhattan's financial district, was a narrow, ugly street lined with brick walls drizzled with graffiti and topped off with coiled barbed wire. Conspicuously absent was anything that looked like an entrance to a theater.

Troy found 323 hand-scrawled onto a green, heavily dinged metal door that looked like it had been plucked off a World War II submarine. Troy knocked, the sound of his fist muted by the dense metal, and after a minute of trying to decide whether to leave, turned the doorknob.

To his surprise, the door was unlocked. He walked up a creaky narrow stairway and pushed his way through a set of heavy red velvet curtains, which snuffed out any remaining daylight that may have breached the cracks of the ancient door, and into blackness.

Standing on a lit stage, whose distance was difficult to gauge, was a lone actor, a Japanese man with an alabaster face, angry brows and red lips. The top of his head was shaved, the remainder of his oily black hair piled into a topknot. He wore two samurai swords of different lengths stuffed into the sash of his white kimono. Brooding notes plucked from a *shamisen* echoed off the walls of the empty theater, magnifying the gravity of the Samurai's presence.

The theater was empty and Troy groped his way into a seat halfway down the center aisle of the theater, never taking is eyes off the actor. Faux snow began to fall and the samurai raised a hand, catching as few flakes. His eyebrows rose in a moment of tenderness, as if had never seen anything so beautiful. He let the flakes spill from his hand.

The tinny notes from the three-stringed guitar were replaced by a solemn voice narrating a few verses in Japanese. A *haiku* of some sort, Troy figured.

As Troy's eyes adjusted to the darkness, he became aware of several human-like forms standing on the stage behind the samurai warrior. He counted three in all, each much larger than the actor, and all dressed from head to toe in black, their faces hidden beneath hoods.

As the samurai knelt down, the three black garbed figures seemed to crowd the actor, two kneeling along with the warrior, like invisible servants, while the third hovered directly over him.

Troy studied the samurai, his proportions somehow off, especially juxtaposed to the black-garbed giants, and he watched how the giants seemed to move in sync with the actor. *He's not real*, Troy thought. The samurai was not an actor, but a puppet, and the black clad figures were the puppeteers, controlling his every movement.

The samurai tossed his katana to the side and laid the shorter *tanto* sword directly in front of his knees. As Troy became engrossed by the samurai's actions, the cloaked puppeteers seemed to dissolve into the background so that only the lone samurai existed.

The warrior placed both hands flat onto the snow-covered ground and bowed deeply. With two hands, he pulled his kimono open, exposing his belly and unsheathed the blade of the *tanto*. Using a two handed grip, he placed the tip of the blade against the left side of his belly. More dramatic notes from the Japanese guitar, and then the Samurai jerked forward, thrusting the blade into his stomach and dragging it across the width of his waist before falling face down into the snow.

Lights came on and Troy had an unobstructed view of the three black-garbed puppeteers standing over the dead samurai puppet. Several people walked out from the back of the theater clapping. The puppeteers each pulled their black hoods off and bowed to each other and to the small group that had appeared, still clapping.

Two of the puppeteers were older Japanese men, while the third was Caucasian, much taller, and silver haired. The two Japanese puppeteers bowed and then receded into the small crowd of admirers who gathered about the taller Caucasian man. The bowing and hand shaking continued on for another five minutes before the tall man excused himself and made his way over to Troy.

"Ah, Mr. Hunter. So glad you could meet me today. Please, sit. Were you able to catch any of the show? Just a rehearsal, really."

"I've never seen anything like it."

The man smiled broadly, displaying perfect, freakishly large teeth.

"It's *Bunraku*. Few westerners have ever been trained in it. The great puppet masters of ancient Japan were trained from childhood. I started rather late in life."

"I've always found puppets creepy."

The man's smile turned into a frown.

"Yes... a common phobia. But, best way to overcome a phobia is to confront your fears head on, right?"

Troy shrugged. He was growing impatient.

"Excuse me, but what is this?"

"I'm sorry," the man asked, appearing not the slightest bit offended.

"Who are you? Why was I asked here?"

The man chuckled as if Troy had made a small joke, and said, "I want to show you something."

Troy followed the older man over to where the puppet hung. Two thirds the size of a man and as lifeless as a bookshelf, it was hard to imagine that minutes earlier Troy thought he was watching a living person on stage.

"This particular puppet, the samurai warrior, is almost three hundred years old. Very few 18th century *Bunraku* puppets can be found in such good condition and almost none exist outside of Japan. I paid six hundred million yen for it, which, at that time, was about two million American.

"In fact, this very puppet was owned by Chikamatsu Monzaemo, the famous Japanese playright, and was used in several of his plays that were performed in front of emperor Higashi-yama."

He reached behind the Samurai's kimono and the puppet frowned at Troy and reached for his long sword.

"The head puppeteer works the head and the right hand, while two apprentice puppeteers work the left hand and legs. In the early 18th century, the height of *Bunraku* it was said to take forty years to reach the level of *omo-zukai*, or master puppeteer. Ten years to master the legs, ten for the left arm, and another twenty for the right arm and head."

"Is that so?" Troy said, unenthusiastically.

"It's the truth. You see, the puppet master is an ironic figure. In some ways, tragic."

He stared patiently at Troy who sighed, but played along.

"How so?"

The old man smiled, his teeth even comically larger than Troy had first thought.

"Because, the better he is, the more invisible he becomes," he said. "All *Bunraku* puppeteers dress in black robes to remain as inconspicuous as possible. Anything, so as not to draw attention away from the puppet, and ruin the magic of the illusion. All, that is, except the greatest masters of all, who were known to wear brightly colored robes."

The man placed a large hand on Troy's shoulder and led him away from the stage.

"Why do you think that was?"

"I assume because they were so talented that nothing, not even brightly colored robes, could distract the audience from the show."

The man smiled and nodded.

"Exactly. So powerful was their art that even their garish colored kimonos could not steel the attention away from the life that he breathed into his wooden puppet. Please walk with me."

"It's an interesting hobby," Troy said.

"No," the man said, wagging a crooked finger. "This is no hobby. You ask me who I am, so I'm telling you. I am a puppet master, and I asked you here because I'm looking for a new apprentice."

Troy laughed and the man chuckled, as well, as if they had just shared a small joke.

"I'm flattered," Troy said, "but I'm not really interested in becoming a… puppeteer. I'm sorry if someone gave you wrong information. Maybe you have me confused with someone else."

The man shook his head. "No, no. There is no confusion. You are whom I asked to meet. But, right now I need to be somewhere. Take a walk with me."

Out of curiosity or boredom, or likely something in between, Troy followed the man. Once out of Theatre Avenue, they turned right onto Ann Street heading towards Broadway, stopping in front of a wrought iron fence that encircled St. Paul's Chapel, one of the oldest standing structures in Manhattan, and the church where General Washington was said to have prayed the morning before his inauguration as the nation's first president.

Troy had walked past the old brownstone church dozens of times but had never been inside. Wedged into a corner of the city financial district and hidden under shadows cast by the World Trade Center, the church was, in Troy's opinion, an oddity.

A chubby policeman standing in the doorway waved at them. The old man returned the gesture. Troy followed him though the portico, past matching Ionic columns and through the doors of the old church. The heavy locks of the massive wooden doors clanked behind them. The strangeness of both his companion and his surrounding left Troy feeling uneasy.

"Did that cop just lock us inside?" Troy asked, trying to sound casual but the concern in voice poorly concealed.

"No need to worry. He's just giving us a little privacy," he said and waved Troy forward. Sunlight sifted through a checkered stained glass window filling the empty pews. Above the altar, a schema of the sun stamped with Hebrew scrawl shot out lance like shafts of light onto the tablets of Moses. And then Troy saw it. He had overlooked it the first time. Lying on the altar was a plain wood coffin.

"What is this?" Troy asked. "Is this a funeral?"

Troy followed the old man to the rear most pew.

"Please, sit with me. I have limited time. The mingling of business and pleasure is a reality of my life. Certainly you can understand that?"

Troy looked around at the empty pews.

"There's no one here."

"The deceased was from the Philippines. He worked for me. A wonderful young man. Sadly, he had no family here, and few friends. I paid for the services, and the rector was kind enough to allow me some privacy to pay my respects."

Organ music filled the chapel startling Troy. The old man closed his eyes and breathed in deeply through his nose.

"Bach. 'Music is good to the melancholy, bad to those who mourn, and neither good nor bad to the deaf.' Do you know who said that?"

"Spinoza."

"Yes, Spinoza. A man who did for morality what Einstein did for physics."

Troy stared at the old man who kept his eyes closed

"I remember you," Troy said. "You were at the memorial for Reverend Jones."

"Yes. I was class of '46. I'm also on the Board of Trustees. I understand you two were close. I'm sorry. I met him once. Seemed like a good man."

"What is this? Why am I here?" Troy asked, now wanting to get away from this strange man and his perverse private funeral.

"You've come highly recommended by one of my closest employees. A former Academy grad as well. Louis Piedmont. I believe you're friends."

"Lou Piedmont. He works for you?"

"Yes. A valuable asset."

"This is a job interview?"

"No, no interview. I have an HR department of a few hundred people that do that sort of thing. Besides, I wouldn't insult you with such a mundane process. That said, I am offering you a job.

"Me, I graduated from Princeton, but I give a lot of money to Yale. It allows me access to potential young talent like yourself. Impressive grades, test scores off the charts, and your evaluations from your professors read like the diary from a school girl with a crush. Yes, all nice. But, it was one comment that got my attention. How was it phrased? '- his knowledge of his subject surpassed only by his knowledge of the audience to which he is addressing.' An interesting observation and perhaps no better a recommendation for what we do in my company."

"And what's that?"

"We are in the business of producing...outcomes."

"I thought you were a puppeteer."

"Metaphorically, yes. Our clients—be it an individual, a company or government– desires a certain outcome. The only thing between our client and the desired outcome is the will of other people."

"So they hire your company to break the wills of those standing in the way?"

The old man laughed gingerly.

"Of course not. That is the business of dictators and fascist regimes. Our job is to bend those wills, not break them. And we do that by studying people, knowing them better than they now themselves. Knowledge is power. There is a Japanese saying. 'A man's fate is a man's fate and life is but an illusion.' *We* provide the illusion. We are the invisible hand, gently guiding the actions of others to the desired outcome. In the end, they must feel that that the decision is theirs and theirs alone. That's the key.

"Lou has told me a lot about you. The kind of things that can't be gleamed from a report card. You're wasting your talents working at that white-shoe firm. You study money, markets, trends. We study people. And I'm going to take a guess that it is people that fascinate you most. Certainly, not money

"I understand that the in a few years you will receive a large sum of money. From, of all things, an anonymous benefactor. How mysterious." The old man chuckled

"How do you know all this?"

The old man made a gesture as if brushing away a fly.

"You see, Troy, we consider ourselves artists People are our medium," the old man said and raised a finger, "but, we are commissioned artists, the outcomes chosen for us by our paying clients. Even Michelangelo's Sistine Chapel was a commissioned work. Sato, the famous Japanese puppet master, was once asked about the secret of his gift. *How was he so effective at convincing the audience that the puppets he controlled were real?* And do you know what his answer was?"

Troy shrugged.

"I don't have to convince the audience that the puppet is real,' he answered, 'but rather, I must convince the puppet that he is real.' You see?"

For the past decade, Nate had relied solely on one form of transportation—his own cab. No buses, no other taxis, no subway, no trolleys or trains. But now, as he squeezed into the tight berth of the Amtrak club car and eased himself into the hard plastic

bench seat by the window, he felt an excitement he had no lon-ger thought himself capable. As the train took off from Montreal Station, Nate's mind shifted to his father, the Pullman Porter, and the magnificent cars he was in charge of maintaining; spacious sleepers fully furnished with cured leathers and Italian fabrics. He wondered what his father would have thought of his current accommodations, the smudged scratched glass windows without curtains; the plastic benches; and the linoleum floors plastered with gum and dirt.

Two hours past and the train began to slow. It meandered through a heavily wooded path lined with tall green pines, their branches sleeved in pristine white snow. A wooden sign with painted carvings of the Empire State Building and the Statue of Liberty welcomed the train to New York.

"Next stop, Rouses Point, New York, USA," a voice announced. "A customs officer will be making his way through the cars. Please have your identification and declaration card out for inspection."

Nate's pulse quickened as he pulled out a copy of his birth cer-tificate, his Quebec driver's license, an old US passport and his customs declaration card.

The customs officer was an old man and he moved slowly with a shuffling step that hinted at Parkinson's. With an unsteady hand he took Nate's papers, gave them a cursory look, checked some-thing off his list and then gave him back his documents minus his declaration sheet.

That was it. Nate was home. No colorful banner stenciled with 'Welcome home Nate!' No flower *lei* necklace. No cake and no one striking-up any band. If this was the beginning of a new life, it sure didn't feel like it.

It was another ten hours to New York City and he reached into his coat pocket and pulled out a folded envelope. He didn't open it, but instead, just held it, pinched in a tight grip as if it were in danger of being blown away by the slightest of drafts.

The envelope contained the note from the boy, hand delivered by the American. Of course, Troy hadn't been a boy for years now, but it Nate's mind, he was still that same child, frozen in Nate's memory on that day, nearly twenty years ago, when Nate said goodbye.

From the opposite pocket he pulled out another sheet of paper, this one brittle with age and held together by several pieces of clear tape. Nate carefully unfolded it and studied the pencil drawing– tiny rectangles stacked like a brick wall. Each brick bore a pattern of sorts. On the bottom of the page, smudged and no longer legible were the words, My Friend Nate.

As a child, Troy had given Nate dozens of drawing during their time together, but the one he now held was the only one that survived. There was something about the picture that irked him, and for nearly two decades, the picture remained a mystery to Nate, as complicated and impenetrable as the boy who drew it.

The drawing had spent the last ten years taped to the dashboard of Nate's taxi, a standing invitation to his passengers to decipher it's meaning, assuming it had one. Although the picture spawned more than a few curious comments, after a decade of staring at the drawing, Nate had concluded that he was reading too much into it. He had finally accepted it the way others did, as the cute but meaningless doodles of a young child. That was, until a year ago, when Nate had picked up a middle-aged man visiting from Boston.

"You're sailor?" the man asked.

"Excuse me?" Nate asked.

"I asked if you were a sailor?"

"No," Nate said, confused by the question. "No, why do you ask?"

"Your picture."

"Nate looked into the rear view mirror and saw that the man was pointing to the dashboard where Troy's drawing was taped.

Nate looked from the drawing to the man in the mirror.

"I'm sorry. I'm not sure what you mean."

The man smirked.

"The drawing. It's a maritime code." The man said, and Nate glanced again at the drawing. Rectangles bearing stripes, crosses, circles.

"They're flags," Nate said, as if seeing the drawing for the first time.

"Yeah. Each flag corresponds to a letter in the alphabet. Sailors would place combinations of flags together on their hoist ropes to communicate to nearby ships. Of course, now days, it's more for show."

Nate eyes shifted from the road to the drawing. He thought of all those lazy days hanging out with Troy on the Berkley pier, talking and staring out onto the water. Troy must have seen the flags on all those boats and just absorbed the code with little thought.

"What does it say? Can you translate it for me?"

The man frowned.

"What's in it for me?"

"I won't charge you for the ride."

The man's brow furrowed as he considered the offer.

"Sure, why not. You got a pen and some paper?"

Troy stared out the window of the Learjet at the darkness below. They were somewhere over the Pacific Ocean.

"Hello, Mister Hunter."

Troy turned to face Ari who held a clear toiletry bag. His face was freshly shaved except for the thick mustache he had been growing for some time.

"How are you, Ari?"

"Very good, my friend. And very excited. I've always wanted to go to Hawaii."

Troy smiled politely.

"Yes, I'm very excited," Ari continued. "*Magnum, P.I.* is very popular where I'm from. I never miss an episode. You know it?"

"Sure," Troy said. "Sure. Tom Selleck. Wears the Aloha shirt, Dodger's baseball cap and drives a red Ferrari."

"Actually, it's a Detroit Lions cap. Yes," Ari nodded enthusiastically. "Ferrari 308 GTS. Look," Ari said, offering his left wrist for Troy to inspect. "Rolex GMT Master. Just like Magnum wears."

"Nice. And the mustache is really filling in."

Ari smiled sheepishly, and gave his mustache a few strokes. Ari's expression turned serious.

"Only one thing different. Magnum carried a Colt Model 1911 .45 ACP. Magnum was in the Navy, so he carries the 1911. I try to like it, but..."Ari wrinkled his nose. "I stick with my Beretta 92. The old man got me a VCR, so now I never miss an episode."

"Is the old man up?"

"No. He finally fell asleep. He sleeps so little. You should try to catch few more hours of sleep. I'll wake you when we're close."

Troy sat on the balcony of the Royal Suite of the Halekulani Hotel in Honolulu, overlooking Waikiki Beach. Further south was Diamond Head, rising up from the clot of white apartment buildings and hotels that hugged the coastline.

He ate banana pancakes and poached eggs with salmon and hollandaise sauce. When he finished his third cup of Kona coffee, he stepped into the massive suite, where several of the old man's staff was busy making phone calls and confirming meetings.

"Where is he?" Troy asked, and a woman talking into a phone head set pointed towards the master bedroom.

The door was open and Troy peaked in. The door to the bathroom was open, and Troy could see the old man leaning over the sink. He was dressed in pajamas decorated with a gold dragon stitched into the red silk fabric.

The old man leaned into the mirror as he flossed. He saw Troy in the reflection and waved him over.

"Macrodontia," he said, as he threaded a new strip of floss through his comically large teeth. "Abnormally big teeth. How is it you never asked me about my teeth?"

"I thought they were caps," Troy said.

"No, no. No caps," he said, baring his teeth and tapping his two front incisors with the nail of a finger.

He tossed the used floss into the sink and inspected his gums and teeth for any spots he may have missed.

"For reasons no one could figure out, my teeth seemed to grow faster than the rest of my body. It wasn't until I started to see double that someone thought maybe something wasn't right.

"I was fifteen when they found the tumor in my pituitary gland. They said it was the size of an almond. The tumor was pumping out growth hormone at ten times the normal rate. It was too big to go up through my nose and get it. They call that *transphenoidal*. Nope, they had to perform a craniotomy to fish it out."

He leaned down and pulled a chunk of hair aside, revealing part of a thin scar.

"I'm so glad you came," the old man said.

"You asked me too. I didn't think it was optional."

"It was the only way I could get you to take a vacation. I have asked Ari to drive you while we're here. He'll take you anywhere you'd like. He's very excited about being here."

"Yeah, he told me."

"Could you grab me my slippers?" the old man asked.

Troy walked back into the bedroom and lifted the slippers from where they lay under the bed. He stopped next to the dresser where the old man had laid out several framed photographs, including one of the old man flanked on either side by Lou and Troy. Troy recognized another familiar face and picked up a 4 x 6 silver framed photograph of the old man seated next to a young Asian man at some sort of formal function. It was Arturo

Bautista, looking very different decked out in tuxedo. He replaced the photo and returned to the old man who had gone back to fiddling with his teeth in the mirror.

Troy laid the slippers on the marble vanity, and said "Don't you have people to help you with those sorts of tasks?"

"A better question is why you agree to indulge this old man."

Troy shrugged.

"You are fatherless, and I am childless. Perhaps, it's as simple as that."

The old man smiled, and for the time, his freakishly large teeth looked sinister. It wouldn't be the last time.

As Troy reached for the door to leave the Royal Suite, it opened. A thin, elderly Asian man with a thinning pompadour and dressed in a three-piece suit of beige gabardine and gold cuff links stepped into the room, along with an entourage of men and women.

Troy moved aside to allow the small crowd to pass, and as he headed out, he heard the old man.

"Ah, Mister President. So good to see you, and looking in such good health"

Stepping out of the lobby, Troy immediately spotted Ari. He sat in the driver's seat of a red Ferrari convertible, wearing a Hula shirt, sunglasses and a Detroit Tigers baseball cap. He waved at Troy and spread his hands in a 'what do you think?' gesture.

Troy sat shogun next to Ari who peeled away from the curve in dramatic fashion. They drove along Ala Moana Boulevard drawing the stares of tourists.

"Where are we going?" Ari asked.

"Turn right at the next intersection."

After ten minutes passed in silence, Ari spoke.

"You are quiet today, my friend. Quiet, even for you. Just enjoying the scenery?"

"Arturo Bautista," Troy said.

Ari looked at Troy as if he had not heard him right.

"Did you know him?" Troy asked.

Ari said nothing for a while.

"A nice young man," he finally said.

"What was he to the old man?"

"The old man loved him like a son. Like he loves you."

"What happened to him, Ari?"

"I don't know. Surely, there are others you could ask."

Troy considered his words.

"Luis. You mean Luis?"

"Mister Hunter, I'm just a driver."

"You are *not* just a driver. Why does the old man hire people like you?"

Ari looked at Troy, his face registering hurt.

"He is a very wealthy man. It's not unusual for men in his position to need extra…security. No?"

"What happened to Arturo?"

"Please, Troy. He is a good boss. He takes good care of his employees. He cares much about you."

"He cared about Arturo, as well. Hell, he had a photograph of the two of them on the dresser in the bedroom of his suite."

"Please, Mister Hunter. Let's not discuss this anymore. Let's have some fun. We are in Hawaii. Look at this place."

"Pull over here."

"But there is nothing here."

"Ari, pull over."

Ari pulled the car onto the shoulder. Troy opened the door and stood up out of the low slung convertible.

"I'm going to walk from here. I won't need your services anymore today."

"Please Mister Hunter…he will be upset if he thinks I abandoned you."

"Don't worry. I'll tell him I made you drop me off."

Troy headed off in the opposite direction. He could hear the engine of the Ferrari growly ferociously as the car sped off.

After a twenty-minute walk, Troy reached the Oahu Cemetery. More like a park or garden, the old Victorian graveyard was unlike any he'd ever seen. No two tombstones were the same and mixed among them were marble statues of angels, gigantic Celtic crosses, and Greek-style reliefs carved into stone columns.

Troy approached an elderly man raking leaves.

"Can I help you?" he asked.

"I'm looking someone who is buried here?" Troy said.

"Well, I think I can help you with that. What's the person's name?"

"Soki Jones. Reverend Soki Jones."

A few dozen papers belonging to Arturo Manuel Bautista, the angelic faced overachieving Harvard grad with a sense of humor, lay scattered over the floor of Troy's master bedroom which remained unfurnished except for a gaudy Tuscan-style canopy bed. Shipped over from Neiman Marcus, the bed had been a gift from Lou and arrived only days after Troy had joined the company.

Troy sat cross-legged on the floor, reading the documents—an incomplete assemblage of memos, market data and receipts extending over a five year period—pertaining to company work done for the J. Rowling International or JRI, as they were called. The company had been hired by the billion-dollar cigarette maker with the purpose of helping them expand their share of the cigarette market in the Philippines. Lack of restrictions on advertising, along with no government mandated health warning on cigarette packages, combined with a corrupt politic, made the Philippines a very desired and potentially lucrative market.

Troy reread a memo from the master puppeteer himself to Arturo tasking him with putting together a strategy of attack that would allow JRI to one day dominate the Filipino cigarette market.

Arturo believed that for JRI ever to have a shot at one day dominating the Filipino market, they would need to start building a rapport with Lucio Tan, the billionaire Filipino entrepreneur and owner of the largest local producer and distributor of cigarettes, Fortune Tobacco. Tan had emigrated to the Philippines from China when he was just a boy and had worked his way through college studying Chemistry in Far Eastern University but quit before graduating. He set up a successful scrap metal business in the late 1950s and later a found a job in a tobacco factory where he was tasked to buy leaf tobacco from the Ilocos provinces.

Using his experience, Tan started his own cigarette company named Fortune Tobacco in 1966. It was also during this time when his close friend, Ferdinand Marcos, was newly elected as President. The tobacco business was a roaring success and by 1980, Fortune Tobacco was the Philippines' largest cigarette manufacturer.

Arturo sent the old man a hefty report detailing just how Lucio Tan became and remained the most powerful cigarette magnate in the country.

By convincing the Filipino Congress to stick with a two tiered *ad valorem* tax system which gave Fortune Tobacco a pricing advantage over its competitors, Fortune Tobacco was able to maintain discriminatory pricing advantages that allowed its international brand names to be classified as local brands, thus reducing tax duties. In contrast, J. Rowling International brand names, manufactured by La Suerte, were classified as imported brands and subject to higher taxes. Arturo concluded that the future success of JRI will depend on joining Lucio Tan. No other way around it.

A potpourri of documents concerning the JRI account gave Troy a rudimentary picture of a campaign aimed at increasing tobacco addiction in smokers between the ages of ten and thirteen. It was to be an assault on children, the largest and most aggressive campaign ever attempted, designed to create a growing generation of smokers who are loyal to the J. Rowling brands.

Running concurrently would be a second campaign to boost the corporate image of JRI by having the company take the high road and shell out big bucks to sponsor everything from schools to sports teams to pediatric wings of hospitals.

The documents were a disjointed sampling from the various pieces of what went into a marketing campaign of this magnitude. There were psychological profiles that attempted to justify the target age. 'The goading and taunting that characterizes the phenomenon of peer pressure at ages 10 to 13 is a narrow window and certainly lost by age 16.' There were gimmicky contests in which empty packages of cigarettes could be exchanged for prizes like *boom boxes* and color TVs.

There was an organized push to increase the quantity of the J. Rowling brand cigarettes being smuggled into the country, since black market sales indirectly funnel profits to the company while putting pressure on the Filipino government to relax its restrictions on imported cigarettes, less associated criminal activity rise. And finally, there were lists of public officials who might be paid off to help lift restrictions on foreign imports.

That Arturo had these documents in his possession was not peculiar. He was the point man on the campaign, hand chosen by the old man. What was peculiar was not what he had, but what he *shouldn't* have had—internal memos and confidential documents from the client company, TRI, documents that were potentially damaging should they ever be leaked.

Why was Arturo hoarding these sorts of documents? Troy knew there could only be one explanation. Arturo was building a case *against* TRI and their marketing campaign designed to build a nation of loyal customers addicted to their product by targeting children.

Maybe Arturo had developed remorse over his involvement in such a blatant corruption of the children of his birth country. Or maybe it was more complicated. Maybe he was plant, sent by the Filipino government to infiltrate the company and expose it from the inside out, or maybe he was acting alone. All unlikely, considering how cautious the old man was. He would have done extensive background checks on Arturo before allowing him into the upper echelons of his company.

At the time, it probably made sense to have a Filipino-American head the marketing campaign, but in hindsight, it seemed to Troy, reckless for the old man who was not one to take chances. Certainly, a man who built his empire on his ability to read others would have seen the inherent risk and potential conflicts of interest in allowing Arturo to head up a project that so blatantly exploited Filipino children. Having never met Arturo, he had to assume that the old man had no reason to doubt that Arturo's loyalty was anything less than absolute.

The little hope he had of discerning Arturo's true intentions lay with the content of several letters exchanged between Arturo and an a man named, Jesus Azurin, who happened to be the Filipino Heath Minister. The letters were mailed to a P.O. Box in Arturo's name and hand written in a strange hieroglyphic-like script which Troy learned was called *Tagalog Baybayin*, an outdated writing system that was displaced by a Latin based substitute when the Spanish colonized the Philippines in the 16th century. It took him a little time, but Troy had found a NYU student who knew the writing system and was agreeable to translate the letters for a reasonable price.

Three hours after the scheduled time of arrival, Nate's train pulled into New York City's Penn Station. Nate sat while the rest of the passengers raced to get their belongings and line up, anxiously awaiting the doors to slide open.

Nate was in no rush. He had nowhere to be and nowhere to go. His decision to buy a ticket and hop on the train was the full extent of his planning. Although Troy had sent him his address, he had no idea if or when Nate might come.

When the last of the passengers had exited the train, Nate stood and calmly collected his bag and made his way out onto the deck.

Two stories underground, the air was stale and made even more oppressive by the low ceilings. Parked against the far wall was a three wheeled shopping cart filled with trash. A dog leash was looped around one of its wheels while the other end was tied to a man's leg, the rest of the body hidden under several layers of clothing and a few soiled blankets.

Hanging above the homeless man was a digital clock displaying the time as

12:47 a.m. Nate thought it felt much later, but in this subterranean world, two stories underground, insulted in a catacomb of concrete and steel, time was something you took on faith.

The sudden smell of urine coming from where the bundled man laid pushed Nate onward and he followed the corridor to a steep stairway flanked on either side by a pair of non-working escalators.

"You look for exit?"

Nate started, not sure where the voice was coming from.

"You look for exit?" asked the voice with a heavy lisp, the accent unmistakably Slavic.

The man stepped out from shadows of a door-sized recess in the concrete and directly into Nate's view. His face was weathered and sunburnt and buried beneath a soot-colored beard. Nate stepped back, recoiling more from the man's smell, the pungent odor of alcohol after it had passed through the liver a few times before being excreted through the pores of the skin.

"I'm good, thank you," Nate said, cutting a wide path around the man.

The man grabbed a hold of Nate's sleeve with surprising speed.

"Which exit you look for? This 33rd and 6th …unless you want subway."

Nate snatched his arm back and quickened his step towards the stairwell.

"I think you lost friend."

Nate looked up to where a second man, equally disheveled, sat on the middle of the stairwell.

"First time in big city?" he said, the accent the same as the first man.

Nate turned away from the stairwell and back towards where the first man stood. Something familiar clicked in his brain and Nate fixed onto the man's mouth, the jagged edges of a harelip thinly disguised beneath the man's dirty whiskers.

The man laughed at Nate's expression of horror as he stared at his deformed mouth. He flashed Nate a big grin. A yellow tooth peaked through the missing flap of skin and Nate shuddered. Fear crept into his chest.

It was over thirty years ago, but Nate saw it as clear as if it were yesterday—the trajectory of his life forever shifted by the man with the harelip. Because of him, he had left Yale, along with his dreams, and crawled back to Oakland with his tail between his legs. Because of him, he adopted the cause of the Panthers, believing only they could snuff out the fear he carried with him like a guilty secret.

But I'm still afraid, Nate thought.

Self-loathing bubbled up from somewhere deep within, filling his gut where fear had already staked a claim. The two primitive emotions mixed in his bowels creating a third, even more powerful emotion—anger. No, not anger. Furry.

No, not this time, Nate thought. *He had ruined my life once. Not this time. Not this time.*

The man seemed to sense the change in Nate and his smile vanished just as Nate rushed him. Nate slammed into the man with his shoulder, and to his surprise, the man buckled, and let out a grunt as Nate landed on top of him. Nate swung his fists wildly at the man's head as he squirmed and flailed his arms about, trying to block Nate's fists.

Nate could see the wedge of missing skin filled with blood.

I'm doing it. I'm winning, Nate thought.

The first two blows barely registered in Nate's brain, the pain dulled into an afterthought by the adrenalin surging through his veins. The third was different. He felt the cartilage between his ribs tear as the blade was pushed deeper into his back. The pain was horrible, well beyond anything he could have ever imagined. He would have sworn that he could even smell and taste the pain, as if his body had decided that the sense of touch alone could not do justice to the magnitude of the insult.

Nate's balled fists no longer raining down on his head, the man with the harelip gave Nate a shove. He rolled off the man and onto his back, landing hard on the hilt of knife. The blade shifted and something inside him snapped, and then he was drowning, unable to get a breath in, as if his head was being held underwater.

Nate's vision began to dim, and he swung his arms about in a futile attempt to reach the knife lodged in his back. The second man leaned down, sticking his face close to Nate's.

"Hurts, don't it?" he whispered. The man stood quickly, lifted his leg up and stomped down onto Nate's chest,

Nate grunted and coughed up a mouthful of frothy blood, and for a moment, he could breathe again.

The man with the harelip appeared, pushing his partner aside.

Standing over Nate, he wiped his nose and mouth with his arm and looked at his bloody sleeve.

Nate lay still. He felt nothing, as if his mind had shed his damaged body, and with it, all pain and fear. A strange calm washed over him. His vision nearly gone, he focused the remaining porthole of sight onto the man's deformed lip, swollen and split open from where his fist had struck.

I did it, Nate thought, as the last of his vision vanished and he slipped into unconsciousness.

❖ ❖ ❖

Through the peephole of his apartment door, Troy studied the photo ID of Detective Anita Gonzalez.

"May we come in?" she asked from the other side of the door.

Troy unlocked the three bolts and opened the door. Both detectives were still holding up their badges.

"Troy Hunter?" the female detective asked.

Troy nodded.

"I'm Detective Gonzales and this is Detective Peterson. We're from the 109th Precinct."

Troy nodded.

"We're sorry to bother at this hour, but we need you to come with us."

Troy nodded.

"Just give me minute to throw something on?"

Both detectives exchanged puzzled looks. Detective Peterson asked Troy, "Ain't you curious as to what this is about?"

Detective Peterson was an older, heavyset man with a bushy mustache and matching eyebrows and thick Brooklyn accent.

"I figure you'll tell me when you're ready. I just need a minute."

Forty minutes later, Troy was at the 109th Precinct, sitting at a small wooden table in anonymous and windowless room. A ceiling mounted video camera, the room's only décor, kept its eye trained on Troy. The two detectives returned carrying three cups of coffee.

"I have one black, one with just cream, and one with cream and sugar," the female detective said, placing all three cups in front of Troy.

"Cream only. Thank you," Troy said.

She pushed a cup towards him.

"I'll take the black," Detective Peterson said, snatching the cup.

Detective Gonzalez took a sip and cleared her throat.

"At just about 1 AM, a body of a man was found in one of the terminals of Penn Station. He was beat pretty badly but his death appears to be due to internal bleeding from a stab wound to the back. Likely, there was more than one assailant involved, based on the pattern of the wounds.

"We recovered very few personal effects. No wallet or ID. No watch or jewelry. We assume the assailants took everything. Since he was found in the Amtrak terminal that services trains from out of state, we assumed he had probably had at least one bag, but no bag was found."

The woman detective placed a clear plastic bag in front of Troy.

"This was one of the few items recovered off the body."

Troy stared at the detective, not wanting to look down but knowing he had no choice. The bag contained an envelope. It was the envelope that held the letter that Troy had paid a private investigator to deliver to Nate three months earlier. It was badly wrinkled and stained pink.

Detective Gonzalez waited for some response from Troy, but when he said nothing, she continued.

"It's just an empty envelope addressed to Nate," the officer said. " Just Nate...no last name or address." She turned over the bag containing the envelope and tapped on the back. "Your name and return address are on the other side. Can you tell us his full name?"

"Nathan Kennedy," Troy answered.

Detective Gonzales began writing.

"K-e-n-n-e-d-y?" she repeated

Troy Nodded.

"Middle name?"

Troy shook his head.

"Where's he from?"

"Montreal."

"He's Canadian?"

"No, he's American."

"When did you see him last?"

"June 3rd."

"Just last week?"

"June 3rd, 1971," Troy said.

Both detectives swapped puzzled looks.

"You haven't seen him in 15 years?" the male detective asked.

Nate nodded.

"Got a birth date?"

"February 9th, 1942."

"What can you tell us about him? Relatives? Occupation? Was he here to visit you?"

Troy ignored the questions.

"Was there anything else? Anything else found on him?"

Detective Peterson looked at Gonzales who nodded. He pushed forward a second clear plastic baggy containing a square sheet of paper held together by clear tape where it had been folded one too many times.

Troy picked up the bag. The tiny rectangular flags had faded over time, the message buried in the flags no longer recognizable. He had wanted to tell Nate how important he was to him, to thank him for saving him from Leon, the Oakland public School System, and for giving him a chance, but he had been too embarrassed. He had chosen to write his note in maritime code, using the colorful flags that decorated the sailboats that soared across the Berkley harbor where he and Nate had spent so many wonderful days. Nate accepted it happily but Troy could tell he had no idea what he was looking at. Troy never told him.

Troy turned over the paper and was surprised at what he saw. Scrawled in pen, in a handwriting that Troy did not recognize, was the translation of his coded message.

Thank you for finding me. I hope we will always be together. Your friend always. Troy.

"You recognize this?" asked the male detective.

Troy nodded.

"You wrote it?"

Another nod.

"When?"

"I was just a boy."

"I'm sorry, Mr. Hunter, but I need to show you a photograph," Detective Gonzales said. "We need you to positively identify the body. Are you okay with that?"

She slid a close up of Nate face, his eyes swollen shuts, his lips and white beard caked in blood.

"Is this Nathan Kennedy?"

"Yes."

"How do you know him?"

Troy picked up the photograph.

"Mr. Hunter?"

"He saved my life once."

Troy stood and handed the picture back.

"Mr. Hunter...Mr. Hunter...we have more questions."

Lou was standing in front of a uniformed female officer who sat at the entrance to the station behind a thick wall of bulletproof glass. He seemed to be having an animated discussion, his arms waving about while the officer seemed barely interested. When he saw Troy, he pointed him out to the officer who rolled her shoulders.

"What the hell's going on? " Lou exclaimed, his normally coiffed blond hair in utter disarray. "I get a call from your doorman telling me you had two cops paying you a visit. You in trouble? You want me to call a lawyer? Should I call the old man?"

Troy flinched at the mention of the old man. He could feel the anger welling up inside.

"Just go home, Lou." Troy stepped past Lou and out into the muggy dawn. Lou followed after him. The morning rush hour was still a couple hours away and the streets were eerily quiet.

"Hey...Troy...I'm talkin' to you. Fuck man! You aren't fifteen anymore. Don't pull this silent, brooding act on me. It's me, Lou. Your best friend."

Troy laughed.

"What the hell does that mean?"

Troy turned to face Lou, who stood with both palms opened helplessly.

"I'm done, Lou. I'm out."

"What are you talking about?"

"Arturto Bautista."

Lou took a step back.

"What are you talking about?"

"Did I ever tell you about when first met the old man? He asked me to take a walk with him. To Saint Paul's Church. You know why? To pay respects to a friend and former employee. Arturo Bautista. The sick fuck had me sit down across from the coffin of the guy I was going to replace. Did you know that?"

Even in wan light, Troy could see the color drain from Lou's face.

"Arturo was the point man on the JRI account. You know that account, Lou. Get Filipino kids hooked on cigarettes. Create a generation of loyal smokers. But somewhere along the way, Arturo grew a conscious. He was talking to the Filipino Minister of Health. I found letters the two of them had exchanged. They were written in some Filipino alphabet that no one uses anymore. That's how scared Arturo was. He was going to blow a whistle on the whole campaign, but the old man got to him first."

Lou said nothing.

"How much did you know? How much did you know when you recommended me as Arturo's replacement?"

Lou's lips parted but no words came.

"You knew the old man was a psycho. You knew what he was about, but you invited your old friend Troy, anyhow. *You* brought me into this shit. There's just one more question I have to ask you.

I just want to know, Lou. Are you the one who tipped off the old man to Arturo's change of heart?"

"Troy…"

"Just answer the question, Lou."

"I didn't know he would…I just thought… I would never have told him if I thought he would…" Lou looked away.

"You fucking asshole."

"Troy, please. Don't leave me."

"Good luck, Lou. You're on your own."

PART FOUR

1990
WASHINGTON, D.C.

roy sat at a rickety table in the rear of an all-night bookstore café in Dupont Circle, pretending to read while watching a silver haired man in an expensive blue suit drag a tiny rake through a Zen rock garden the size of a paperback novel. He dragged the toy rake slowly, eyebrows clenched and the tip of his tongue slipping out the side of his mouth like a child trying to color within the lines, the rake just a sand's grain away from personal *Feng shui.*

Like misery, loneliness loved company, and Troy could always find plenty of that in big cities—strangers packed into bars and coffee shops at all hours of the day, seated shoulder to shoulder but pretending not to notice each other. He learned quickly that being alone in a big city was a lot less lonely than being alone in a small city, and he had learned to appreciate the company of strangers.

What brought Troy to Washington, D.C., he couldn't say. It was just the next stop in a growing list of American cities that Troy called home at one time or another, never intending it to be his last stop. Like everywhere he had lived, he arrived knowing no one and his first days in the nation's capital were spent riding aimlessly about on a 90cc moped purchased from a Georgetown University graduate student. He bought a fold out plastic map of the city and

130

studied it for a few seconds before handing it back to the puzzled street vendor who sold it to him.

Washington D.C was a city of artificial borders. On a map, it's perfectly straight boundaries created a perfect geometric figure that defies geography. An imaginary line separates D.C. from Virginia and Maryland. More imaginary lines further divide the city into four quadrants, named for compass points with the epicenter being the Capitol. It didn't take Troy long to realize that these lines did not only designate changes in street names from North to South, or East to West, but also demarcated changes in race, class, and culture. Georgetown, the affluent predominantly white area of D.C.—home to ambassadors, professors, and politicians—resides in the northwest. In the opposite quadrant, the southeast is as different as night from day.

For the past two weeks Troy had grown increasingly restless, wondering if it was time to move on, and at the same time concerned that his stays in each new city were growing increasingly shorter. And then there was Jenna.

The relationship was a mere few weeks old—Troy's longest in many years. He had first seen her at the *Barnes and Nobles* in Georgetown. She went there after work at the same time every day. She bought the same things—a bottle of Perrier and a shot of *expresso*—and she sat in the same seat in the rear of the bookstore's café.

The fourth time Troy spotted her, she had just finished paying for her drinks and was carrying them to the rear of the café when she saw someone already seated in her usual seat. She stopped for moment, unsure what to do. She surveyed the café for open seats, and for a moment, Troy thought she might take the open seat next to him. But just then, the older man seated in her usual seat stood to gather his things and Troy could see the relief wash over Jenna's face.

Jenna had stirred Troy's memory of a young Panther girl who served breakfast at St. Michael Church, back when he was just a child living with his mom in Oakland. Unlike the girl from the St. Michael's Church, Jenna's hair was straightened, but they both shared perfect skin and bodies that were curvy and athletic at the same time.

As she sat across from him, Troy found himself engaging in the childhood trick he rarely did any more—spinning and unfolding. He lifted her in his mind and rotated her, seeing her beauty from every perspective. When he was satisfied, he froze the image and then began unfolding it so he could see her from every possible angle and all at once. Like a supercomputer performing thousands of simultaneous calculations, Jenna unfolded in Troy's mind in seconds and he gasped, startled by her perfection.

His old friend Nate had once asked him what it looked like in his mind when he 'unfolded' people. Troy didn't know how to answer him back then.

"Is it like looking at a person through a kaleidoscope?" Nate asked, and Troy shook his head. It was nothing like a kaleidoscope, which takes an object and distorts it into symmetrical patterns that have nothing what so ever to do with the actual object. A kaleidoscope does nothing to get its viewer closer to the truth; just the opposite, in fact. But back then, Troy didn't have any comparison to offer Nate.

Now, years later, he could have explained it better. He would compare the 'unfolding' of a person to the intimate knowledge one has of a lover. The difference was this. It might take weeks and months and sometimes longer to learn every inch, bend and curve of a lover, much of the journey navigated in the dark, by touch. But when Troy 'unfolded, it was intimacy achieved at warp speed.

He approached Jenna that day in *Barnes and Nobles*—just walked right up to her and introduced himself. He surprised himself by how much he wanted her and how much he needed her to like him, feelings he thought himself incapable of. Although he did not show it, he was self-conscious of his clothes and embarrassed by his lack of possessions and his tiny unfurnished apartment. He wooed her with the only thing he had, his mind, and like many beautiful and smart women, she was drawn to his intelligence.

They had known each other for only three weeks, but spent every evening and all of their Saturdays and Sundays together.

He closed his book, a worn copy of *The Divine Comedy* in its original Italian, and stuffed it into in his knapsack, and within minutes was riding his moped down the proud tree-lined streets of Georgetown, which quickly gave way to the anonymous grey office buildings of the deserted business district. He reached Washington Circle and was completing his third rotation around the empty park before a taxicab muscled him out from his orbit and onto Pennsylvania Avenue, towards Capitol Hill.

In silence but for the high pitched monotonous whine of the bike's small engine, Troy rode on, past the government buildings, monstrous slabs of glowing white marble, deserted and quiet, like a graveyard for giants.

He smelled the sewage water before he could see the lights flickering off the murky surface of the Anacostia River as he approached the 11th Street Bridge. One moment he was in the nation's capitol, and the next he was in a wasteland of boarded up row houses, the streets teeming with people, like zombies from some low budget horror flick, moving with no obvious purpose and no rational destination. Abandoned cars lined the streets littered with broken glass and last week's trash. Of the traffic lights that worked, a persistent blinking yellow light emitted the stern warning, *yield*.

The plastic map of the city that Troy had memorized in seconds did not include Anacostia, and Troy coaxed the small bike through the narrow neighborhood streets guided by sheer impulse. He recognized the names of the streets, a *who's who* of famous abolitionists and Civil War generals. It was clear that more than the river, it was years of neglect and poverty that had isolated Anacostia from the rest of the capitol, and turned the capitol's first planned suburb into a warzone.

On a corner lot, flanked by brick row houses of crumbling *Italiante* detail and failing front porches, stood a building unlike the others, except that it, too, stood in various stages of decay. A mansion *a la* gothic revivalism, a style he had seen in so many public libraries or Eastern universities, built from rough-cut stone of contrasting colors. Standing at the center of the mansion, like an architectural exclamation point, was a massive tower with a conical roof decorated with needle spires. On either side of the tower were two giant windows, deeply recessed into walls of stone and framed by round arches.

There was something resigned about the tower, crooked and hunched, like an old man, and Troy felt an immediate affinity for the mansion, so out of place here in this urban wasteland of boarded-up apartment houses, liquor stores, and check cashing shops. He wondered what Ruskin would have said about the house.

A cast iron fence adorned with rusted grape vines encircled the mansion. Troy leaned his bike to the left and popped the kickstand open, hopped off, and walked up to the spear tipped gate and gave it a tug. It started to swing open before catching on a green plastic-coated bicycle chain curled around the base. Something moved to Troy's left, startling him, and he stumbled backward landing hard on his bottom. He sat frozen, watching the façade of the mansion, feeling the gaze of another but seeing nobody, and when nothing happened, he jumped back onto his bike and took off down the street without looking back.

It was one AM and Troy stood across from the same abandoned mansion he had stumbled on the two days earlier. There was a strong breeze and Troy listened to the sound of a newspaper being dragged along the floor before wrapping around the foot of an iron bench where the bundled form a person lay. Troy took aim at the façade of the hotel, focusing the barrel of his Nikon lens with the tiniest movements of his wrist.

Unlike the previous night, there was a tremendous amount of activity outside the old mansion, and as he stared through his camera, again loving what only the lens could offer—intimacy without closeness, participation without responsibility.

He locked in on a young woman breastfeeding an infant through an unbuttoned man's shirt (*click*). Like a sniper chambering the next round, he advanced the film with a quick flick of the thumb. She was standing over a man in his early twenties who sat on the cement, shirtless and barefoot, clutching a brown-bagged bottle. The man was a dejected parody of a drunk, shaking his sunken head from side to side while the woman spewed insults at him with mind numbing speed (click).

A man who had been sleeping under a green blanket a few feet away peeked out to see what all the commotion was about (*click.*). A couple of young pushers who were watching the whole scene from across the street shrieked with glee with each new barb from the young woman.

That same night, Troy returned to his apartment and grabbed all the unused rolls of film he could find and placed them in his backpack along with his Nikon and extra batteries. He changed into a clean black T-shirt and jeans and tied his black canvass Chuck Taylors. He slipped on a green pullover from GAP, a gift from Jenna. It still had the tags on and he plucked them off and tossed them onto the ground. He pulled out his wallet and thought for a moment before slipping it under his mattress.

It was a weeknight and 2 AM, the street out front of his studio apartment was quiet. He walked across to a payphone on the corner and fed it a dime before dialing Jenna's cell phone number. He knew she turned her phone off after she went to bed and Troy waited for the answering machine to pick up.

"It's me, Troy. Something's come up. I need to go away for a bit. I think I found a story. Shouldn't be more than a week...tops." He thought for a moment and then added, "I miss you."

Troy awoke to the sound of a child singing and for a moment he couldn't remember where he was. He opened his eyes but didn't move. After his eyes began to adjust to the darkness, Troy gingerly pushed himself up into a sitting position, very conscious of having grown weaker over the past weeks from a combination of muscle atrophy and hunger. He listened but the singing he heard in his sleep was gone. It was unusually quiet, and Troy figured it must be dawn since that was always the quietest time of the day.

In the beginning, it was not noises but the smells that most bothered Troy. The addicts never showered. Sweat and dirt clogged their pores preventing their drugs from seeping out of their skin thus prolonging the high. No one ever told the children to take a bath, nor would they have listened had such a demand been made on them. But excluding the crack heads and the children, most of the inhabitants of the old mansion, Troy included, never washed themselves simply because there was no running water.

Weeks had passed since Troy had last showered and the smell of his own body no longer bothered him. There were too many worse odors to occupy ones attention. Mold, weed, feces, and vomit—their scents mingled in the stagnant air like a witch's potion. And then there was the most noxious smell of them all, like burning plastic, but worse. It wafted down the halls and oozed from the ceilings—anywhere crack was being smoked—the horrible smell managed to find him.

Troy used the side of his hand to sweep away the dust bunnies that had begun to encroach onto the space he had claimed for himself in a small room on the third floor. It had taken him hours to clear a suitable space in the debris—broken glass from smashed crack pipes, syringes, dust balls, candy wrappers, crushed cans and white plastic bags. The bags were small, opaque sandwich-sized baggies with concentric red circles stamped on the side—the logo used to identify the product as coming from a specific dealer.

Troy heard singing again, this time coming from just outside his room. He stood and walked to the door, the floorboards squeaking with each step. Stale air seeped into the room as he pushed the door open. Troy peeked out into the hallway and spotted the figure of a small girl seated a few yards away. Her body swayed back and forth as she sung. Troy recognized the melody of "Twinkle, Twinkle Little Star" but the words were unfamiliar and ad-libbed. Troy walked up to the girl and knelt down next to her. He had not seen her before. She had one pigtail sprouting from the side of her head behind her right ear, and on the other side, instead of a matching pigtail, there was an angry patch of red skin.

"Hi," Troy said.

"Shh!" the girl reprimanded with a finger over her lips. "You gonna wake 'em."

Troy looked around but saw no one.

"Who?"

"Them," she said, pointing to three black roaches lying on their backs.

"How do you know they're sleeping?"

"'Cause. See there… how they're on their backs. You see how their little arms and legs move all twitchy. That's cause they dreaming. My little sister did that. She move like that when she sleep."

"I see," Troy said. "So, what do you think they're dreaming about?"

"Well, once, in school, the teacher read us this book about these bugs who lived in this big peach, so I think that's what they's dreamin' bout. Just livin' in this giant peach, eatin' all they want and floating 'bout in space."

"That's probably it," Troy said and the little girl eyed him suspiciously at first but when she was satisfied that he was not making fun of her, she smiled.

"Where is your sister?" Troy asked.

The girl shrugged and started to sing, a different song, which Troy didn't recognize.

"May I take a picture of you?"

The girl looked at Troy.

"You got a camera?"

"I do."

She thought for a moment, her right hand drifting up to the side of her head where the pigtail was missing.

"I guess so? They was gonna take pictures of us in school but we had to leave before they did."

"It has a flash so it's gonna be kind of bright, but don't be scared."

Troy snapped three shots.

"Wow, I see spots," the little girl said, blinking and grabbing at the air in front of her.

"Can I try?" She asked.

Troy looked around, making sure no one had snuck up on them. He showed her how to hold the Nikon, one hand under for support, the other on the side ready to snap and reload. "You just hold it steady and look right through there with one eye."

"I'm gonna to take your picture now," she said, trying on serious tone. "Now don't move. Say cheese."

Troy smiled and played along. The flash popped and Troy wondered how long it had been since someone had taken his picture.

Troy constantly worried about his camera. The first thing he did when he snuck into the old mansion was search for a suitable hiding place. In a small empty room on the third floor, which was probably used as servants quarters a century ago, he found a loose floorboard that popped up easily and offered a perfect hiding place for his backpack.

He retrieved the backpack, but kept the camera hidden, withdrawing it only for a few seconds to get the shot he wanted less someone see him. There was no sense giving anyone yet another reason to murder him while he slept. He snapped a few more pictures of the little girl and thanked her.

Most of the regulars who made the mansion their home were either addicts or suffered from mental illness and Troy had managed to photograph most of them. Aside from these regulars, Troy observed a steady stream of people who came and went at all hours. Hookers with their Johns in tow, searching for some privacy; wandering addicts looking to shoot up or smoke; and then there were the runners, young boys in gold chains and brand new leather high tops. They wore bulky winter parkas and baggy jeans with plenty of pockets and they carried two or three pagers apiece. They came to drop off cash and pick up more drugs and then it was back to the streets, always keeping a tight schedule, the same runners arriving and departing at the same hours of the day.

On several occasions, Troy observed the runners pass through the foyer and library before making their way back to what was once a kitchen before disappearing through an inconspicuous door that lead to a part of the hotel that was sealed off from where Troy squandered away the hours.

The door was metal but painted in a half-hearted effort to not draw attention. It hung from massive steel hinges and looked like an expensive custom job. The façade of the door was heavily dented and encircling the heavy metal handle were BB sized pockmarks left over from a repelled blast of a shotgun. Scratched in the paint was a warning 'Abandon all hope. Ye who enter here.' And beneath it, a logo of concentric red rings, the same logo he'd seen stamped on the white baggies which littered the floors.

Troy recognized the quote, plagiarized from the transcription on the entrance to hell in Dante Alighieri's 14th century poem, *The Divine Comedy*. He counted the rings, nine in all, like the rings of hell.

A tiny red light drew Troy's attention and he looked up to see a mounted video camera blinking at him from the corner of the ceiling. Troy smiled dumbly at the camera, hoping to appear stoned and harmless.

Another week passed and to Troy's surprise, he was still alive, although he seemed to have caught a bug. He was burning up. He had stripped down to only his jeans but would have gladly shed them as well if he weren't worried about a surprise visit from one of the mansion's less savory guests. The last few days were spent holed up in the same small room where he hid his camera. Although he had not left the room, the mansion felt strangely deserted and he heard and saw no one in many days, his only company being the voice in his own head. The weaker he became, the louder the voice grew until it drowned out the sound of his own hacking cough that ate away at his sleep. It talked all night long, chattering nervously about random subjects—history, art, movies. It recited long passages from novels and Shakespeare's sonnets. It sung off tune—everything from commercial jingles to operas to show tunes.

"Troy," the voice pleaded, but this voice was different than the one that had taken up refuge in his skull.

"Troy. You got to get out, Troy!" the voice begged. Troy opened his eyes.

"Nate?"

Nate kneeled over Troy. He had his black beret pulled low over one eye and his brown leather jacket buttoned to the collar.

"You need to leave. You're better than this, Troy. You don't belong in Oakland."

"But I left Oakland, Nate. I did what you told me."

Nate didn't respond.

"Nate?" Troy repeated. "Why did you leave me, Nate?"

Nate stood and adjusted his beret.

"Nate, don't go. Please. I need you. I didn't want the money. Just don't leave me again."

He smiled down at Troy and turned to leave.

Several pairs of hands grabbed Troy, lifting him off the floor. Someone held him in a bear hug while another lifted his feet off the ground. Even had he possessed the energy, resisting would have been pointless and he watched as a young man knelt down and began digging at the floorboards with the shaved head of a screwdriver. He was skinny, maybe no more than fifteen, and he wore a bandana on his head, tied to the front in the style of Tupac.

Finally, he popped up one of the floorboards and pulled out Troy's backpack and flashed Troy a mouthful of gold.

He held Troy's Nikon, caveman like, and shook it as if he had no idea what the strange black object was.

"What is this shit?" he said, digging around in Troy's backpack.

"He's a narc," another voice said from somewhere beyond Troy's line of sight.

The arm hooked around his windpipe tightened, and Troy clawed at it, struggling to breathe. The arm relaxed just enough for Troy to suck in air.

"Is that right? That what you is?" the gold grill asked, poking Troy in the chest with the screwdriver.

"Man, he ain't no narc," said a third voice. "I know DEA. He ain't DEA. Shit, he look like some dumbass tourist. Just drag his ass in there like you was told."

Troy's wrist and ankles were duct tapped and a pillowcase was thrown over his head. He was lifted off the ground and carried like rolled carpet down two flights of stairs and through several doorways. For a moment, they had stopped moving and Troy could hear the twisting of metal gears as several locks were opened and then they were moving again. As Troy was being carried, he marveled at the size of the mansion, realizing that he had probably only been in half of the livable space. Finally, they stopped and Troy was dropped into a seat where he stayed, bound and blinded.

"What the fuck is this?" a man asked, his voice deep and mature, unlike the other three.

"You said bring him, so we brought him," answered the teen with the mouth full of gold.

"Jesus, lose the hood. He looks like a fuckin' klansman. Gives me the willies. And lose the tape. Shit, the nigger's been livin' here for the past month. He's barefoot and sick as shit. Where the fuck you think he's goin'?"

The tape around his wrists and ankles were cut and just as the sheet was pulled from his head, Troy lurched forward, his chest seized by a fit of coughing which left him lightheaded. For a minute, everything went black. His vision slowly returned as oxygen reached his brain and Troy looked around the room. He was alone now except for the man in charge. Troy's eyes felt watery and hot, and he blinked rapidly, trying to get them to focus.

"Looks like kennel cough. Probably, got the runs too, huh?" said the man, who was seated behind a metal desk. He was older, late fifties, wiry, wearing a powder blue matching Nike warm-up pants and jersey. He grabbed a bottle of Wild Turkey off the edge of the desk, twisted off the top and handed it to Troy who shrugged it away.

"Suit yourself," he said, taking a long swig. The man looked Troy up and down, shaking his head.

"I knew it was you. Didn't want to believe it, but I knew. Fuck...me!" the man spat and walked back around the desk. "I believe this is what you educated folk call *irony*. Troy Hunter, here in the same shithole as me. Just another worthless nigger—no better than the crack heads and *hoes* you living with. Yep, looks like the joke's on me."

Troy stared hard at the man. The years had stolen muscle and he gained a smattering of new tattoos and scars, but there it was, on his shoulder, faded and distorted by time. *Pater Pacavi.*

"Marvin" Troy said, his mouth so dry the words barely audible.

"Uh-uh, Troy," he said, shaking his head. "It's Dante now. I ain't been Marvin for a long time."

Troy opened his mouth to speak but instead coughed up a large gumball sized chunk of bloody phlegm, which he spit onto the ground.

Dante cringed.

"You dying, boy. I know death when I see it. Troy fucking Hunter, sittin' in my house. Only thing missing is a big red 'Return to sender' stamped on your forehead."

Troy rubbed his tongue around the inside of his mouth, searching for saliva.

"What are you talking about?" Troy asked.

Marvin's eyes lit up and, for a moment, Troy could see the fierceness that he remembered so many years ago when Marvin had first rescued him from a beating he was taking in a deserted back alley of the Combat Zone.

'All we, like sheep, have gone astray; we have turned everyone to his own way; and the lord hath laid on him the iniquity of us all.' Marvin recited. "What's it from, Troy?"

Troy shook his head.

Marvin pulled out a chrome-plated revolver and pointed it at Troy.

"What's it from, bitch? Don't play dumb with me, boy."

Troy looked from the gun and then back to Marvin.

"The Bible," Troy whispered.

"Book and verse, mothafucka?" Marvin barked, pulling back the hammer.

The door burst open and the three boys who had delivered Troy filed into the room, guns waiving in the air.

"Yo, Dante. You want me to *cap* this bitch?" the grill said.

"That ain't gonna be necessary. This here is a family squabble, ain't that right, Troy? Troy here ...we go way back. Shit, he might as well be my son."

The boys glared at Troy, clearly disappointed that no one was going get *capped*. They stuffed their guns back into their pants.

"You sure you good boss?"

"Get the fuck out," Marvin snapped. "I ain't paying you to hang here with your dicks in your hand."

The three teens closed the door behind them.

Troy cleared his throat, and said, "Isaiah 53:6."

Marvin smiled and lowered the gun.

"That's right. Hell, Troy, you a goddam genius." Marvin said, and laughed. "Hell, you know everything. Gifted. Special. Anyone could see it. Shit, even a criminal pimp like me could see it. Saw it the moment I laid eyes on you in that alley all those years ago. Even as that hillbilly biker was woopin' your ass, I seen it. Marked on your forehead, clear as Cain. When I found you, I thought—this is it. This was my chance," Marvin said, slapping his chest for emphasis. "God was sending me a chance."

"What are you talking about?" Troy said.

Marvin face grew grave and he spoke slowly and deliberately.

'*You will open their eyes and turn them from darkness to light,* God says, *and from Satan's control to God's. Then they will receive forgiveness for their sins and a share among God's people who are made holy by believing in me.*' Marvin repeated. He smiled, his eyes alit by the promise of the words.

"I'm talkin' about redemption, Troy. A second chance. You!" he said, pointing a finger at Troy. "*You* were supposed to be my redemption. The Bible says '*something good from something bad.*'"

Troy's eyes widened and Marvin smiled, nodding.

"The money," Troy said. "The anonymous benefactor. That was you."

Marvin slumped back into his chair.

"And look what my money bought me."

"I never asked you for nothing. I never asked to be anyone's savior. Especially some crazed drug dealer."

"Watch it, boy." Marvin snapped. "You in my house now."

"I didn't ask to be anyone's savior," Troy repeated.

"No? Well, don't worry. That you aint! Certainly weren't your mama's savior, that's for sure."

For a moment Troy said nothing, unsure if he had heard Marvin correctly and Marvin smiled.

"What did you say?" Troy said, his voice hoarse and strained.

"I look into my investments. I like to know where my money is going. I wanted to meet the woman who brought the 'chosen one' into this world. Yep, I learned all 'bout you. Like how you left your mama to rot while you went on to bigger and better things."

"Shut up," Troy said weakly.

"Don't even know how she died, do you?"

"Shut up."

"But I do, Troy. I know."

"You're lying.

"You know I'm not.

"You mother fucker," Troy screamed, grabbing the gun off the desk and leveling it at Marvin's head

"Yeah, that's it," Marvin said. "Now you a bad ass, just like me. A street nigger with a gun. A thug."

"Shut up."

"I went out to Oakland. I needed to see her for myself. Pay my respects to this amazing woman who brought me a second chance. It wasn't easy to find her, but I did. I thought I was gonna meet the Madonna," Marvin said with a laugh. "Imagine my surprise when I found her sucking dick for money so she could buy blow."

Marvin shook his head at the memory.

"Was probably a nice lookin' lady before she lost all her teeth. I introduced myself. Told her I knew her son. That you was gonna do great things one day and that she should be real proud. But she wasn't listening. Just kept insisting that she needed you. Needed to see you. Wanted me to bring her to you. Wouldn't stop begging."

"But I knew it wasn't the right thing for you," he said, shaking his head. "No way. You didn't need baggage like that."

"You're lying," Troy whispered. His eyes swelled with tears.

"I mean, I couldn't possibly let her," Marvin went on. "I was protecting you, Troy. You didn't need that shit in your life. Would've dragged you down faster than cement boots. So…I gave her the next best thing." Marvin pulled out a white baggy from his pocket and waved it in front of Troy.

"I watched her shoot up with my best shit. She must've been using some low quality Mexican crap. Don't think she was used to my quality. I watched as her eyes rolled back into her head. Watched as she OD'd in some shithole that makes this place look like the Ritz-Carlton. And I did it for you, Troy. All this, I did for you."

Things seemed to move in reverse. The plaster wall behind Marvin's head, dull and colorless, one second, was now awash with an odd marbling of colors—red, white and black. Next, a perfect black hole, as thick as a pencil, appeared just above Marvin's right eye, followed by the blast, and finally, the gun jerked wildly in Troy's hands, nearly escaping his grip. Marvin's body swayed for moment, and then tipped over, disappearing behind the desk.

Troy stood frozen. He could smell the spent gunpowder in the air. A painful ringing noise reverberated in his skull, and he turned the gun towards the door, expecting Marvin's crew to burst through any second. He waited for what seemed like minutes but they never came.